LOYAL TO THE SOIL 2

Jibril Williams

**Lock Down Publications and Ca$h
Presents**
Loyal to the Soil 2
A Novel by *Jibril Williams*

Lock Down Publications

P.O. Box 944
Stockbridge, Ga 30281
www.lockdownpublications.com

Lock Down Publications
Like our page on Facebook: Lock Down Publications @
www.facebook.com/lockdownpublications.ldp

Book interior design by: **Shawn Walker**
Edited by: **Kiera Northington**

Stay Connected with Us!

Text **LOCKDOWN** to 22828 to stay up-to-date with new releases, sneak peaks, contests and more…
Thank you!

Submission Guideline.

Submit the first three chapters of your completed manuscript to ldpsubmissions@gmail.com, subject line: Your book's title. The manuscript must be in a .doc file and sent as an attachment. Document should be in Times New Roman, double spaced and in size 12 font. Also, provide your synopsis and full contact information. If sending multiple submissions, they must each be in a separate email.

Have a story but no way to send it electronically? You can still submit to LDP/Ca$h Presents. Send in the first three chapters, written or typed, of your completed manuscript to:

LDP: Submissions Dept
P.O. Box 944
Stockbridge, Ga 30281

DO NOT send original manuscript. Must be a duplicate.

Provide your synopsis and a cover letter containing your full contact information.

Thanks for considering LDP and Ca$h Presents.

Jibril Williams

Chapter 1

"Yo E-Moe! Go get the bucket of water. This bitch nigga thinks shit sweet," Velli said with a wicked grin on his face. Velli had been bringing the streets of D.C. nothing but straight havoc since he came home from prison 24 years ago. Velli had been seeking revenge on his childhood friend, Stone, for sending him to prison for nine long years.

E-Moe came back with a 5-gallon bucket of water filled halfway to the rim. Velli knelt down in front of Stone's top right-hand man, Bugga.

"Listen slim, this beef has nothing to do with you. All you go to do is give the nigga Stone up," Velli said to Bugga. Blood ran from Bugga's right side of his head and mouth. His right eye was completely shut. Taking in a deep breath, Bugga hog spit in Velli's face.

"Death before dishonor nigga!" Bugga uttered out of his mouth.

Velli just smiles as the glob of spit and blood rolled down his face. Velli admired the dude's heart and loyalty. They don't make dudes Ford tough anymore. Most niggas crack under such pressure. He snatched Bugga's shoes and socks off and placed his feet in the water while Bugga struggled to get free.

"Man, look I got money. Just let me go slim. I got that bread," Bugga said rethinking his present situation.

"Naw tuff nigga. It's death before dishonor remember?" Velli said attaching the jumper cables to the steel bucket that Bugga's feet were in.

The end of the cables was hooked to a diesel battery with a kill switch on it. E-Moe stood behind Velli with his eyes glazed over from the PCP he had been smoking. He watched

Velli's every move. He was a psychopath when it came to torture and killing. The smile that he had on his face revealed that the show Velli was putting on was a good one. Standing six feet tall, his lanky frame was covered with tats and his dreads came down to the middle of his back. E-Moe was the worst type of nigga, the quiet storm type. The kind that would eat at your mother's dinner table and kill your ass an hour later.

"E-Moe, gag this nigga."

Without hesitation, E-Moe picked up one of Bugga's socks that was right next to the bucket. Smiling at his victim, E-Moe slammed a left hook into Bugga's chin, knocking his head back. E-Moe stuffed the sock in Bugga's mouth.

"Do you know why you are going to die?" Velli asked Bugga as he knelt down in front of the switch, ready to send 25,000 volts through Bugga's body.

"The nigga that you going to die for tonight is a rat; the worst type of disloyal motherfucker!" Velli yelled.

E-Moe just smiled as he saw nothing but terror in Bugga's eyes.

"You sitting here protecting his whereabouts while he's somewhere hiding like the rat he is. You think he's going to avenge your death?"

Bugga tried to say something, but Velli ignored him and hit the switch on the battery. The 25,000 volts fiercely struck Bugga's body. His eyes bulged out of his head as his body stiffened. E-Moe grinned harder at the effects of the shock torture. Velli hit the kill switch, shutting off the battery. Bugga's body slumped in the chair. The way that Bugga's chest heaved up and down Velli knew he was still alive. Snatching the sock out of Bugga's mouth, Velli just stared at his victim.

This is your last chance. Where the fuck is Stone?" Velli asked in his most humbling voice.

Bugga began to cry, and a thick clear glob of saliva oozed from his mouth.

"Man, I swear to God I don't know where that nigga at!"

"Oh yeah, so you telling me and this crazy ass nigga that's here with me that Stone's right-hand man doesn't know where Stone lives or where he be at? Okay have it your way," Velli said getting ready to place the sock back into Bugga's mouth.

"HOLD UP! HOLD UP!" Bugga begged Velli to stop.

"He fucks with this Spanish bitch that stays out in Iverson Towers in the apartment complex. I don't know what apartment she stay in but I do know the building."

Hearing this Velli's insides lit up with joy. Finally, Velli got a line on this nigga Stone.

"Man, I don't believe you," Velli said trying to soak up all the intel he can from Bugga.

"Man, I'm telling you what the lick reads. I dropped the nigga off out there a few times," Bugga tried to plead his case.

"Alright I believe you, but where is the stash house?" Velli questioned.

"Man promise me you won't kill me," Bugga negotiated for his life.

"Okay you got that but think about what you going to tell me because I need all the truth coming from you," Velli said making eye contact with Bugga.

"3730 S. Street Southeast," Bugga blurted out. "That's where the coke is stashed. No one but me, Stone and his brother Mookie knows about the house."

"So, there's no one guarding the house?"

"Yeah and no. There are two old heads that stay there all the time. Stone pays them to sit on the coke. It's a man and woman that be there."

"What about the money?"

Bugga put his head down. Velli hauled off and slapped him.

"The money nigga!" Velli was getting impatient.

"18th and Monroe Street Northwest. Three times a day money be dropped off to be counted up at the end of the night. The money be picked up, moved and dropped off to another location."

"A'ight. Thanks, slim." Velli started to walk away from Bugga. "Trash him!" Velli gave E-Moe the order.

"Hold up! I thought you wasn't going to kill me!" Bugga cried.

"I'm not, he is," Velli's said pointing to E-Moe who was standing there with a devil's grin on his face.

Just then E-Moe pulled out his blue steel 44 bulldog and put Bugga into eternal sleep with one shot to the head.

Chapter 2

Muhammad and his little brother D-Money pulled into the parking lot of Tampa's infamous strip club, "Hollywood Nites" off of Howard Ave. The parking lot was full of the city's finest hustlers climbing out of their old school Chevy Caprices and Caddies sitting pretty on 28- and 30-inch rims. D-Money's gold Lexus with the black Ashanti rims wasn't a sight for sore eyes either.

"Damn bruh. Look at all these bitches out here my nigga," D-Money said, admiring a bow legged shawty pulling her Louis Vuitton luggage and checking into the Hollywood Nites for her shift.

"Yeah Money I see them," Muhammad said feeling a little uncomfortable.

Muhammad just came home two days ago off an eight-year bid from the Feds. He was doing a fifteen-year sentence but thanks to Obama passing the new crack law and allowing crack offenders with no violence attached to their cases a two-point reduction in their sentence, Muhammad was released early. Strip clubs weren't Muhammad's thing, but it had been eight long years since he touched or saw a woman naked in all her glory. D-Money handed Muhammad a stack of bills.

"Bruh that's all you right there," referring to the money he just gave Muhammad. "I want you to enjoy yourself. Welcome home," D-Money said with sincerity.

Muhammad respected the hell out of his little brother for his actions and love that he showed him since he came home. Stepping out of the car Muhammad looked flawless in his black Gucci shirt and white cargo linen shorts with Gucci slip on loafers to compliment his attire. The rose gold iced out diamond necklace with the matching pinky ring set everything off and made him project the image that he was getting money

11

just like the rest of the niggas that invaded Hollywood Nites parking lot.

D-Money had been getting money in Tampa for the last two years. He hooked up with an OG by the name of Biggz through a mud duck (an ugly girl with a bangin' body) named Tyesha they were both fucking. It turned out that Biggz was the man in Tampa. He took a liking to D-Money and put him up under his wings. The money had been rolling in ever since for D-Money.

Making their way to the entrance of the club, D-Money dapped up a few niggas that he knew. Muhammad saw that his little brother was respected and that made him feel a little more comfortable. Rihanna's hit single, "Pour it up," could be heard coming through the club doors. D-Money knew those strippers were in there tearing those poles down as they danced and twerked to Rihanna's sexy and enticing voice.

Walking inside the club the scene was live. Hollywood Nites was something special. The women were the thickest and the finest that the city of Tampa had to offer.

"Daaaaaamn bruh, you see that bitch right there! Shawty got ass phatter than a Mississippi mule," D-Money said, getting hyped and grabbing his crotch as the stripper worked the pole on stage in her purple thong and bare titties. Her nipples were rock hard, and they looked like Hershey kisses. Her 44-inch ass swallowed her thong. What really highlighted the stripper was how her body glistened like she was dipped in a bottle of Johnson and Johnson baby oil. Shawty on stage worked the pole like she'd been training to be a stripper all her life.

Muhammad couldn't focus on just one stripper. His lustful eyes wouldn't let him do so. Everything with titties and an ass his eyes were on it.

"Man, these bitches in this motherfucker," D-Money said with his crotch in his hand.

"Man, who you telling! "Muhammad agreed.

Walking over and finding a corner booth, D-Money ordered two bottles of Cîroc and pineapple juice. Muhammad wasn't big on drinking, but he was going to do his thing tonight while celebrating being a free man. D-Money saw some niggas he needed to rub shoulders with to advance his hustle to the next level when the opportunity arose.

"Yo big bruh, I see some people I need to holla at. You think you can hold shit down until I get back?"

"Yeah Money I can do that, but you need me to step with you though?" Muhammad asked.

"Naw bruh everything is Gucci," D-Money said sliding out the booth and grabbing one of the bottles of Cîroc and making his way over to the people he was trying to plug into.

Muhammad sat back in the booth and watched his brother's politics. The Weeknd's joint "Earned It" blared through the club speakers. A light skinned chick crawled onto the stage like a seductive cat stalking its prey. Niggas went crazy. They threw money on her before she even came out of her cat suit. Muhammad's view was cut off by the 5'5 goddess that stood in front of him.

"Big daddy you want a lap dance?" the eye candy said seductively making eye contact with him.

"Hell ya!" Muhammad said, pulling the large stack of bills from his pocket and handing her a $50 bill. "Do ya thang lil mama," Muhammad coached the stripper.

The chocolate goddess went straight to work working her body to the rhythm of the music. Instantly Muhammad became hypnotized with the way that this woman moved in front of him. Nothing in the room existed except for him and the young devil that released the lustful beast that laid within him.

She reached forward grabbing the back of Muhammad's head gyrating her wide hips in front of his face. Her pink thong was so tight you could see the imprint of her clit through them. Her abs flexes with every move. Grabbing a handful of her thighs Muhammad just had to touch the softness of this woman.

Knocking his hand away shawty whispered, "No touching," as she turned her round ass to Muhammad, not missing the beat to the music. She bent over grabbing her ankles and made her ass shake without moving and inch of her body. Pulling her thong to the side revealing the nicely shaved loved box, Muhammad's manhood instantly got hard. He reached out and stuck a finger inside the stripper. She worked his fingers coating them with her juices. Sliding off his finger and straddling him as the song ended she whispered, "Didn't I tell you no touching?"

"Yeah you did," Muhammad said smelling her sweet musk that coated his fingers.

"Well then that's going to cost you another $50."

"How much is it going to cost to get the shebang?" Muhammad asked getting a closer look at the stripper's face.

"$300 and I need my cash up front and we can go into the back in the dressing room."

Recognizing the stripper Muhammad couldn't believe who was sitting on his lap.

"How about I give you $1,000 if you just spend the night with me. I just came home off an eight-year bid from the Feds, and I can use some companionship."

Thinking the offer over the stripper agreed to spend the night with him.

"A'ight. My shift is over anyway. Let me get my shit and I'll be right back."

"Oh, before you go shawty what's your name?"

"Oh, it's Keke," the stripper said walking towards the dressing room walking a walk that demanded all attention.

Check Out Receipt

Woodlawn Branch
410-887-1336
www.bcpl.info

Friday, November 18, 2022 4:02:47 PM
75217

Item: 31183210354483
Title: Loyal to the soil 2 : a novel
Call no.: Fiction WIL
Due: 12/9/2022

Total items: 1

You just saved $14.95 by using your
library today.

Free to Be All In
No late fees for overdue items
Ask for details or visit bcpl.info

Chapter 3

Muhammad was getting his money's worth out of Keke as he slammed into her from the rear filling her love box up to its fullest capacity. With her back arched Keke yelled out in pain and in pleasure. She hadn't had her pussy worked over like this in a good little while. She enjoyed every stroke and thrust Muhammad put on her.

"Damn this just coming home dick isn't a joke," Keke thought to herself. Big daddy was taking eight years of pinned up sexual frustration out on her pussy and Keke loved every minute of it as she threw her ass back on her punishers rod.

"OOOOOOOH! Yes big daddy! Work that dick!" Keke moaned as Muhammad gripped her round ass tighter.

What was overwhelming to Keke about this guy's lock stick wasn't the length it was only seven inches, but the width on that bad boy had to be thicker than a large cucumber. Seeing Keke bouncing back on his glistening love stick was too much for him. He felt the climax building up in his sack and his manhood expanded to its maximum. He was ready to release and as he banged harder into Keke he let out a lion's roar.

He pulled out of Keke and spilled his load allover the soft skin of her back side. Breathing hard Muhammad looked down at Keke as she laid on her stomach enjoying the twitching feeling that danced in between her thighs still covered in Muhammad's juices.

"Mmmmmm that was the bomb," Keke said sucking on her bottom lip looking over her shoulder at the man that just blew her back out.

Muhammad said nothing. He just threw on his boxers and white cargo shorts, grabbed the bottle of Cîroc off the cheap Motel 6 table and stared at Keke. Muhammad was 38 years old with a medium build and his 5'8 frame was compact. His hazel eyes gave him a sense of charm. His eyes were what attracted so many women to him and rocked so many niggas off their square of defense.

Feeling the vibe change in the room Keke asked, "Are you okay big daddy?"

"Yeah baby I'm fine. Let me go get you a wet washcloth and towel so you can clean up." Waling into the bathroom Muhammad closed the door behind him. Turning the water on and dropping one of the washcloths from the towel rack into the sink, his thoughts started to run.

"That's definitely her. Her face has healed well. I'm going to find out what happened to my daughter." Lathering the washcloth with the cheap motel soap that the motel provided, Muhammad turned the water off, grabbed the washcloth and towel and exited the bathroom. He handed Keke the soapy washcloth and towel.

"Thank you big daddy," Keke smiled as she took the items from Muhammad. He watched her as she wiped the thick love syrup off her and slid into a pair of lace boy shorts. Muhammad asked his question.

"Keke do you know who I am?"

Hearing this made Keke realize that she didn't even know this nigga's name and she just let him dig all inside her guts without any protection.

"I'm sorry baby I didn't catch your name," Keke said trying not to look embarrassed.

"Oh, don't trip!" Muhammad played the game. "You can call me Steve, but you know me as Muhammad.

"No, I don't think I know you."

"I'm the Muhammad that just spent the last eight years with your husband Dinkles Abdule Hakeem."

The hairs on Keke's neck stood up when she heard her husband's name. She didn't recognize him without his long beard and his black and white Kufi that he was famous for wearing. She couldn't believe that eight years in prison could change a person's appearance so drastically.

"Muhammad, how you get out?"

"Call me Steve. Muhammad is no longer me. It's not important how I got out. What's important is what the hell happened to my daughter A'idah."

Keke put her head down hearing baby A'idah's name. Her devil's mind started to work.

"Keisha! What happened to my daughter?" Steve snatched her up by her arm and used the name that he truly knew her by.

"It's not my fault," Keisha cried out trying to loosen Steve's vice like grip. "It was your own wife and Malaya that got that girl murdered." Keisha was lying through her teeth. "It was their doing that got your daughter killed. Let me go Muha-whatever you call yourself now and I'll tell you what you want to know."

Steve let Keisha's arm go but still stood over her with hate in his eyes.

"Spill the beans before I break your neck," Steve threatened.

"Your wife, Anya and Malaya," Keisha wiped her eyes, playing the role as she began to spin her vicious web of lies. "They started selling drugs for this nigga named Mike that used to hustle in Tampa."

"What?" questioned Steve as he stood still over Keisha.

"Yeah they were making runs for him to try to get some money together for Velli's legal defense."

"Bitch you lying!" Steve grabbed the bottle of Cîroc and sat next to Keisha on the bed.

"Anya wasn't selling drugs to get Velli no legal money," Steve said in disbelief.

"Malaya sold drugs to get that legal fee money, but Anya hustled to pay for the medical bills that baby A'idah accumulated from fighting cancer."

"My daughter didn't have cancer Keisha." Steve's anger was mounting.

"Yes she did. Anya never told you."

Steve was not believing what was coming out of Keisha's mouth.

"How did my daughter get killed Keisha?"

"Some stick up boys robbed Malaya's house thinking that the nigga Mike was stashing money at her house. They robbed the house and killed A'idah because Malaya and Anya wouldn't tell them where the money was at."

Avenging his daughter's death was on Steve's mind. No one who partook in his daughter's death would live. Keisha laid the icing on real thick.

"I was going to tell my husband what was going on but before I could do so Anya and Malaya jumped me and cut my face up and broke a few bones. I was I a coma for months. I even lost an eye Steve," she said grabbing and hugging him.

Steve heard about the attack on Keisha but never knew who was behind it.

"Steve I know that you are going to seek revenge about A'idah, and I want to be with you when you do. I have info about Malaya and Anya," Keisha said as she kissed Steve's lips putting her plan into play.

Chapter 4

Malaya woke up to the chiming of her clock, notifying her that it was time for her to offer the Fajr prayer which is best known as the dawn prayer. She reached over to where Velli, her husband, slept only to find his sleeping space was cold and empty. "Pssss!" Malaya let out a long sigh of frustration, realizing that she just spent another night in an empty bed. Muzzling the clock, she sat up in bed. "Where is he?" she thought to herself.

For the last few years this was her story. Waking up to empty beds, dinners without conversations and many lonely nights. In the beginning Velli would fly in from D.C. to Florida every other week to spend that hubby and wifey time with her that she craved so much. Those days were long gone. Malaya would be grateful if she could get a few days out of the month with Velli. She hadn't physically touched him in ninety days. It seemed like the life he lived in D.C. had swallowed him up whole. Malaya was afraid that she was losing Velli to the streets again, even thought it was her actions that got him there.

If she would have never gotten into the game three years ago she would not be on this emotional roller coaster today. But Velli would still be locked up in a federal prison if she wouldn't have gotten in the streets and got that money to get her husband out. Thinking about the situation in depth, Malaya shouted out, "I should have killed Mango's fat ass when I had that blade jammed in his neck!" "Something's got to give," she thought to herself.

Mango was really what was keeping Velli in the streets and away from home, forcing Velli and his brother Damu to keep his flow of drug money rolling his way after he found out that Velli and Damu killed one of his biggest distributors on the east coast named Mike. Mango interrupted Malaya and Velli's wedding day with his goons, threatening and demanding that Velli would be his next east coast distributor or suffer the consequences by having his whole family wiped out in front of his eyes on his wedding day. Making the deal with the devil, Velli agreed to move the work. Velli would set up shop in D.C. and since Malaya and Anya's names were ringing in Tampa they introduced Damu to everyone that was buying from them. Now Damu got the Tampa city on lock.

Malaya placed her feet on the floor and stretched her 5'1 frame trying to get the morning sleep out of her bones. She headed to the bathroom to release her bladder. Washing up for the morning prayer, Malaya stared at herself in the bathroom mirror. Her almond brown eyes stared back at her with such sadness. Her black hair fell down past her shoulders to the middle of her back and even without a drop of makeup at 5:15 in the morning, Malaya was still drop dead gorgeous. She exited the bathroom and entered into the smallest room of the house that she and Velli dubbed as the prayer room. Standing in the middle of the room facing east towards Mecca, Malaya began to recite the opening chapter of the Qur'an in Arabic.

A small figure appeared beside her, somewhat startling her. Two-and-a-half-year-old Tiriq, her nephew, joined Malaya in her morning prayer. Even though he had been muted ever since he was born, he always followed behind his auntie and mother while they performed their five daily prayers. Since the day Tiriq was brought into this world, Malaya had spent a lot of time with him. She was like his second mother.

Malaya wanted a child so bad, but she refused to bring a child into this world without Velli being home full time. Finishing up her morning prayer with Tiriq, Malaya sat down on the floor and contemplated the oneness of Allah with Tiriq beside her with his head resting against her arm.

"Good morning Tiriq," Malaya greeted her nephew. Tiriq just stared back at her with those big brown eyes like his mother Anya and a smile just like his father Damu. At the age of two and a half, Tiriq didn't talk or cry out loud. The doctors said that there was nothing physically wrong with Tiriq that prevented him from talking. They advised Anya and Damu that he would talk when he was good and ready.

"You want some Captain Crunch Berries Tiriq?" Malaya asked rubbing his peanut shaped head. Before she could get all the words out her mouth Tiriq's little head was bobbing up and down.

Tiriq sat in front of the tv watching his favorite cartoon, Spiderman, and enjoying his cereal. Malaya's phone started to ring. Seeing that it was Velli facetiming her she hit the talk button and his handsome face appeared on the screen of Malaya's iPhone 6.

"As Salaam Alaikum beautiful," Velli greeted his wife.

"Wa laikum Salaam," Malaya mumbled.

"I see that even at 5 something in the morning you are still a beautiful sight to see."

"Thanks," Malaya said playing Velli's comment to the left.

"Okay I see that's what it is. Baby I'm sorry that I did not make it home last night, some things came up."

"Velli you haven't been home in three months!" Malaya snapped.

"I know baby some important shit came up."

"Yeah more important than me right?" her words cut into Velli like a sharp blade.

"No baby, nothing is more important than you," Velli said trying not to get upset with his wife. "I will be home in three days I promise."

"Three days!" Malaya pouted her lips. "Baby just let me fly into D.C. and spend a few days with you please!" Malaya begged.

"No. Shit is too dangerous right now. I'll be home in three days. Just give me three days baby."

Malaya was silent for a minute just staring at her husband on the screen of her phone.

"Okay Velli. You got that. But in three days that ass better be here or I'm flying to D.C. No permission asked."

Velli just shook his head and made the deal with his wife.

Chapter 5

Velli disconnected the phone with Malaya with his mind and heart in turmoil. Being away from his wife for such long periods of time was starting to take a toll on him. Spending nine long years in prison away from Malaya was a total nightmare. Many nights he stood in prayer asking Allah to not place a burden on him that he couldn't bear and return him to his wife. In the strangest way those prayers were answered, and Allah brought him home to Malaya. But after being home two and a half years he felt he was farther away from his wife now then he was when he was in prison.

But he owed everything to Malaya. It was because of her that he had the opportunity to walk the streets again. The things she had to endure for him caused him to relive murderous thoughts. Just the thought of Mike and Keisha's treachery, drugging, and raping Malaya, brought his blood to a boil. Even though Mike was resting in an eternal sleep-in hell for his actions, Velli still thought the chump got off too easy.

Velli couldn't believe that Malaya had to watch Anya's nine-year-old daughter, A'idah, get murdered in front of her and still was mentally sane today. Velli laid his head back on the sofa and took a deep breath.

"Man, this shit got to end soon," Velli thought to himself. "I got a lead on this scary ass nigga Stone, I got to capitalize off the info I got from Bugga," Velli thought running his hand over his hair studded bald head.

He had been on a mission. He'd been slowly building a strong team around the Washington D.C. area trying to cut off Stone's money flow. Thanks to E-Moe's knowledge of a few people out in Maryland, he was able to take over Capital Heights, Seat Pleasant and Silver Springs, Maryland. Velli had been locking down smaller blocks throughout the city but just as always some dudes were loyal to Stone because of the consistency that he brought to them in the drug trade. Others had betrayed Stone and switched connects just because Velli's prices were cheaper, and the word was that their coke was running neck and neck on quantity. Velli's goal was to kill Stone, dry the city out, then flood D.C. which would automatically put him in the position to be king of the city. But his plan hadn't been that easy until he ran into Bugga. Now the city was about to heat up and become the thrones for Velli and E-Moe.

Chapter 6

Anya walked through her and Damu's four-bedroom house in Wesley Chapel, Florida in a powder blue lace thong and matching bra set. Her 5'9 hourglass frame moved gracefully as she walked on her all-white plush carpet. Entering the kitchen her loving husband Damu sat at the kitchen table enjoying the morning paper and consuming an egg and toast sandwich. Even though Anya was a southern girl from Georgia she loved her husband with his city swagger.

"Salaam (peace) hubby. You know Tiriq's going to kill you when he finds out you drank all his apple juice," Anya said opening the refrigerator and grabbing the orange juice out of it.

"Sal-," Damu stopped speaking in mid-sentence captivated by his wife's nakedness. The color of the powder blue thong set she wore highlighted her golden complexion and walnut brown eyes.

Anya was every man's desire. There was only one man that was capable of handling her and that was Damu.

"Salaam love. I see that you know how to greet your husband in the morning," Damu said with a sexual undertone in his voice.

Anya gave up her innocent little girl smile and played along with Damu.

"What are you talking about? I always know how to greet my husband in the morning, noon and night." Anya winked at Damu, standing wide legged, giving Damu a glimpse of her slightly shaved bush that could be seen through the front of her lace thongs.

Damu burst out laughing at the performance his wife put on for him, walking over to her and placing his arms around her waist and firmly taking a handful of her back side. Feeling her softness melt into his hands he became furiously aroused. Looking into her eyes he confessed his love for her.

"Anya Williams I adore everything about you." He placed a soft kiss on her lips.

Anya's love box became wet as she took her husband's tongue in her mouth. Damu and Anya had been married for three years now. The loss of her daughter, A'idah and her divorce from her now ex husband Muhammad brought her and Damu together. Situations and secrets they would both go to their graves with had built them a bond that was more intricate than Bonnie and Clyde. Damu helped Anya seek revenge on her child's killer and in the process unveiled a dark secret in Damu's past that led to his deceased wife's killer. They were a match made for each other. Still kissing Damu broke loose.

"What's your plans for the day before we even get started?" he asked while grinding his lips into Anya drawing attention to the hardness that was budging out his jeans.

"MMMMM," Anya moaned meeting her husband's sexual gesture. "I have to go to the office to meet Malaya. We have five consultations with authors that are trying to get BAM Publications to publish and market their books. I have to go pick up donuts and coffee for the soon to be clients."

"Well, there's no need for us to start something we can't finish," Damu said releasing Anya from his grasp.

"You just make sure you are home early enough tonight so I can put some of this good loving on you."

"Oh, I most definitely will." Damu smiled at his wife.

"I almost forgot," Anya said walking over to the table and taking a bite of Damu's unfinished egg sandwich. "Malaya is bringing your son to the office. Could you stop by and bring us some lunch? Besides you know Tiriq would love to see you."

"Yeah baby I could do that. Is there anything that you want in particular for lunch."

"Yeah, fried fish and a salad will be fine baby," Anya said, taking another bite of Damu's sandwich.

"Okay I will be coming through around 12:30, after I come from hollering at Biggz," Damu said as he walked over to Anya taking his half-eaten sandwich out of her hand and kissing her on the lips. He walked out the kitchen to go conduct his worldly affairs.

Jibril Williams

Chapter 7

The traffic in Ybor city near the downtown Tampa area in the am was no joke. The sidewalks were full of suits and khakis of corporate workers hustling to make it to work on time carrying espressos in one hand and briefcases in the other. Steve sat on 7th Street across form BAM Publications, the business establishment of Anya and Malaya. It was a corner office building with a small parking lot that sat next to it. It was a white two-story building with large window fronts with the name BAM Publications over the top of the building. Just looking at the building let Steve know that Malaya and Anya were eating good or was this the benefits of them robbing and killing Mike? Steve thought to himself. Keisha told him everything he needed to know about Anya and Malaya's shady asses, robbing and setting niggas up. Steve shook his head just at the thought.

"Anya must be back up to her old tricks," Steve spoke out loud to himself.

He was there to approach Anya and question her about their daughter's medical condition. For the life of him, Steve couldn't believe that Anya would withhold that type of information from him pertaining to his daughter. Steve watched the office of BAM Publications like a pimp watched a hoe on the hoe stroll. Finally seeing the white Range Rover pulling into the parking lot next to the office building, Steve hopped out his car and made his way across the street to the parking lot where the truck just pulled in. Anya was talking on the phone to Malaya and didn't see the approaching figure.

"Okay I just pulled up to the office right now. As soon as Neva gets here I will ask her about finishing the editing work for Jibril and Malika's next book," Anya said to Malaya through the speaker phone.

"Okay did you get the donuts and coffee for the new clients?" Malaya questioned on the other end of the phone.

"Girl I got it," Anya giggled, "you act like I work for you," Anya joked with Malaya.

"Girl don't play. I just want things to be on point and official looking when our client steps foot into our establishment. That's all girl no offense."

"I can understand that" Anya replied back, grabbing her Prada bag off the floor of the passenger side.

"How far are you Malaya?"

"Mmm… about twenty minutes out. Me and Tiriq stopped and got apple juice from McDonald's."

"That boy and his apple juice. Oh shit!" Anya said as she saw Steve ten feet away from her truck.

"What's wrong Anya?" Malaya questioned, getting alarmed at eh seriousness in Anya's voice.

"Muhammad is here. I'll call you back." Anya disconnected the call.

Retrieving her pepper spray from the console between the seat, Anya placed the small canister in her lap and rolled her window down. She knew that seeing Muhammad without wearing his long beard meant that he had strayed from his Islamic teachings. A flood of emotions hit her like a ton of bricks. She cared for this man, but she hated him with the same heart, if that was even possible. When Steve found out Anya was raped he disowned her and threw her to the curb like trash, but she loved him because they one had something special together, A'idah, their deceased daughter.

"As Salaam Alaikum!" Anya greeted him.

"Hi Anya. I don't do the Islamic thing anymore," Steve said staring Anya in the eyes. Sitting there in her Hijab (Islamic head wrap), she just shook her head at his statement.

"What brings you here Muhammad?" Anya was still clutching her pepper spray.

"It's Steve now. No more Muhammad."

Ignoring his statement Anya asked again, "Why are you here?"

"Why? You think Damu is going to find out that I've been here?" Steve said trying to get a reaction out of her.

"No, I'm not worrying about my husband finding out you've been to my place of business. He is a very secure man." Anya clenched her jaw tighter hating that she said that to Steve. Anya couldn't help but to feel sorry for Steve. After all, she had been married to this man for ten years. It was not easy seeing a person you once had a life with seem so lost.

"Husband? So, you married Damu?"

Putting her head down Anya answered Steve.

"Yes I married him. Remember you didn't want me anymore."

Steve acted like he didn't hear the last part of her statement.

"Did you give him a child Anya? Do you love him?" Steve asked taking a step closer to her truck.

*****

Neva pumped her brakes hesitating to turn into BAM Publications' parking lot. She kept driving until she got a few blocks away and pulled over in front of a Starbucks. She hit the speed dial on her phone. The ringing of the phone could be heard throughout her Lexus speakerphone.

"Hello," a sleepy voice answered the phone.

"Keisha this is Neva," Neva yelled.

"What's wrong Neva?" Keisha could hear the panic in her cousin's voice.

"It's that fuckboy ass boyfriend of yours, Steve. His stupid ass is at the office talking to Anya in the parking lot."

"What?" Keisha said jumping out of bed.

"Keisha this fuck nigga going to fuck everything up that we worked so hard to do," Neva complained.

"Go see what you can find out and I'm going to try to call him."

"Okay Keisha but we might have to put our plan into effect sooner than we thought," Neva said.

"I know," Keisha said disconnecting the call.

*****

The question Steve asked Anya made her eyes glaze over with tears that threatened to fall.

"Yes I gave him a child and yes I'm madly in love with my husband." Anya lifted her head up and made full eye contact with Steve.

"You gave that nigga a child, but you couldn't even let me know that my daughter was dying of cancer? You robbed me of saying my proper goodbyes to my daughter Anya!" Steve said with spit flying out of his mouth.

Anya was shocked that Steve knew the secret that she had kept from him for so many years. "Who in the hell has he been talking to?" she thought to herself.

"I'm sorry but at the time I thought she was going to get better, and I didn't want to worry you. Hell, I didn't know how to tell you that our daughter was dying. How do you tell someone something like that?" Anya shouted with tears running down her face.

"I guess it's no reason for me to be here," Steve said as he turned to walk away.

"Steve!" Anya called stopping him.

"What!" Steve said turning around to face Anya again.

"Do you need anything? Money, clothes?" Anya asked.

Steve just gave Anya a smirk and walked away. As he was walking out the parking lot Neva was pulling into the parking lot. They both made eye contact.

Chapter 8

Watching the two chicks laying on the floor in front of the floor to ceiling aquarium feasting on each other's pussy was a sight for Stone. He slowly stroked his erect penis while enjoying the freak show from the comfort of his couch.

"The square root of sixty-nine is ate something," Stone said out loud laughing at his own joke.

Inhaling the Atimo stuffed with Cali the most potent purp that the West Coast had to offer, Stone licked his lips as the dark-skinned stripper named Splash slurped on Peaches' clit while jamming her middle finger into her center piece. Peaches let out a moan that brought Stone to a hardness that he hadn't been able to abstain in months. Not wanting to deny himself any longer he commanded the two lustful women to come and share their tongue action on his throbbing manhood.

The two beauties crawled over to where Stone was sitting. Peaches being the one eager to please she grabbed Stone's eight-inch manhood and engulfed it in her mouth making sure the tip of his manhood touched the back of her throat.

Stone opened his legs wide and slid his ass to the edge of the couch so Splash could place his nuts in her mouth while Peaches worked her mojo on his dick with her tongue.

"SSSSS...that's right bitch. Work that dick. Eat them nuts," Stone coached.

Peached sucked and slurped harder applying more saliva every time her head went up and down Stone. Stone laid his head back on the cushion of the couch and let Splash and Peaches lick and suck his frustrations from the day out of him His phone began to ring as it laid beside him on the couch. Peached tried to reach for the phone but her hand was knocked away while she still held Stone captive in her mouth. Seeing that it was his brother Mookie he had to answer it.

"What's up Slim?" Stone answered the phone.

"Man, I think that nigga Velli done got his hands on Bugga," Mookie said from the other end of the phone.

"What makes you say that?" Stone said placing his hand on the top of Peaches' head guiding her head to a slow pace.

"It's just a gut feeling Stone. Nobody has seen Bugga in three days and we found his car parked on Good Hope Road over southeast about two hours ago."

"Naw I think that nigga is laid up with one of them freak bitches that live over there on Good Hope Road. He'll pop up soon," Stone said with confidence.

"Okay what we going to do about Velli?" Mookie said getting a little frustrated at his brother's lack of concern for Bugga's whereabouts. "The money's starting to decline, and niggas is jumping ship on us switching suppliers and buying their shit from Velli and that nigga E-Moe," Mookie complained.

"Is shit still jumping hard on the Southside and in the Northeast?" Stone questioned.

"Yeah but we lot all that money that was coming in from uptown. Velli got that shit on smash. And what's this shit I hear about you supposed to have told on Velli?"

"Man fuck that nigga Velli. I never told on Velli. Let his bitch ass eat," Stone yelled sending vibrations through his and to the women that were still sucking and licking on him. "I'm about to retire from the game in about ten months," Stone said through the phone. "I had a good run so it's time to make my exit and live somewhere on a white sandy beach."

"So, you just gonna run from Velli like some bitch and leave me here to deal with your demons?" Mookie said testing his brother's gangsta.

"Mookie, who the fuck you think you are talking to?" Stone said sitting up on the couch making his nuts pop out of Splash's mouth.

"Stone, I don't mean to offend you, but I just don't want to deal with Velli when you disappear. I just want to keep getting this money so one day I could retire," Mookie said sincerely.

Stone had mixed feeling about the Velli situation. Velli was his childhood friend, they both ran the city of D.C. almost eleven years ago. Stone gave the police a tip on a murder that led to Velli doing nine years in prison. Even though he didn't testify on Velli he knew the rules to the street. Once a rat always a rat. Once Velli was locked up Stone thought Velli was going to give him full control over the city by turning him on to the connect but Velli gave the connect to his brother Damu. This didn't sit well with Stone, so he put a price on Damu's head with a young gun by the name of Mike. Mike took the contract but once he went to fulfill the contract Damu wasn't anywhere to be found. Out of frustration Mike killed Damu's wife Crystal instead. This turned out to be a good idea because that forced Damu to retire out the game and flee to Florida to take care of Velli's wife Malaya.

"Hello?!" Mookie asked from the other end of the phone.

"Yeah slim I'm still here," Stone said breaking his thoughts and turning his attention back to Mookie on the phone. Splash and Peaches were still working his private area.

"So, what we gonna do about Velli?" Mookie asked again.

"If the nigga does something drastic before I retire I will send the twins to rock him to sleep. Either way I'm going to kill Velli."

"Alright. That's what I'm talking about," Mookie said getting hyped up.

"But in the meantime, locate that nigga Bugga."

"Alright Stone I gotchu. Oh yeah have you seen my baby mama Splash today?"

Stone looked down between his legs where Splash had a mouthful of nuts and said, "Naw slim I ain't seen the bitch," and he disconnected the phone.

Chapter 9

Velli felt good being back in Florida, even though it was only going to be for a few days. He was hoping that these few days were going to get him over the hump of missing Malaya. Most of all the thought of him going back to prison was haunting him daily. Going back to prison was something he couldn't afford to let happen. He was going to have to put his big boy plan down soon before shit really heated up in D.C. Stepping onto the curb of Tampa International Airport, the sun warmed Velli's skin. Even though he was only 6'2 he carried himself as if he was seven feet tall. His freshly shaved head shined in the Florida sun. He was dressed in blue jean shorts, an all-white Polo shirt and a Polo belt that hung loosely around his waist. The fresh Timb's that Velli rocked unlaced gave him a GQ urban look. The transitional Polo glasses complimented his light brown complexion. Spending many years in prison and putting his body through all those intense workouts had paid off for him as his arms flexed against the Polo tee that he wore as he clutched the overnight Prada bag that was slung over his shoulder. Seeing Damu's red Range Rover with the jet-black rims pull up in front of him Velli broke out into a smile. Jumping into the truck Velli gave his brother some dap and a hug from across the passenger seat.

"As Salaamu Alaikum Bruh!" Velli greeted his little brother and true crime partner.

"Wa Laikum Salaam! Man, I missed the hell out of you."

"Likewise little bro. How's the family?" Damu seemed hesitant.

"Anya is still the love of my life; Malaya is still the best sister-in-law the world but she just missing you and wants you to put an end to the situation in D.C." Damu went on. "Tiriq is looking and acting like me by the day and the other day I swear he was going to speak his first words to me," Damu began to get excited.

"That's what's up bruh! I'm glad that everything is Gucci in the sunshine state, and I see that Tampa is treating you good. I taught you well," Velli said checking out the 2015 Range Rover he was riding in.

"Yeah Tampa is treating a nigga okay. The publishing company is starting to produce some figures from what Anya and Malaya tell me. How is shit going in D.C.?" Damu said looking over at his brother.

"I just got a good line of information on that nigga Stone. I'm going to move on him in a few days when I get back to the city. After that I'm going to set E-Moe up with my man Ken-Ken that I met in the Feds which will be the new connect. I will be getting 15% of the take E-Moe makes in the city. From there I will be bringing my ass home to move on Mango fat ass and get ghost with my family."

"Shit bruh we can move on Mango now. Everything is in place for that," Damu said checking his rearview mirror.

"Naw hold fast. We still need his coke to do what we need done in D.C."

Damu nodded his head up and down in agreement. Velli and Damu drove a while in silence. Damu decided to drop a bomb on his brother.

"Yo Velli, you know that nigga Muhammad is home?"

"Muhammad who?"

"The Muhammad that was married to Anya the one you were so close with in prison."

"How you know this Damu?" Velli asked with a seriousness in his voice.

"He paid Anya a visit at the publishing company."

Velli put his head back on the soft leather of the truck's headrest, closing his wyes and letting out a sigh.

"What did he say? What did he want?" Velli said keeping his eyes closed.

"That nigga really don't want shit. He just asked Anya about A'idah having cancer."

"How did he find that out?" Velli asked opening his eyes.

"Man, I don't know. That nigga even asked Anya about me and her being married to me. He even asked about her having a child with me."

"Damu, it's obvious that Muhammad has been talking to someone that knows about A'idah's cancer situation. Do you know where the connection lies?"

"Naw bruh I don't know. I wish that I did though," Damu said checking his side mirror.

"I wonder how he found Anya," Velli said wiping his hands over his face.

"Shit bruh that wasn't hard for him to find out. He must have found out through BAM Publications. You know Anya and Malaya did publish several books right? You know how niggas be in jail reading them urban books from front to back. So, I figure that's how he found Anya seeing as though he showed up at the BAM Publications office building."

"Yeah you probably right with that one Damu," Velli said still not believing he was out and located Anya. "Did he ask about me?"

"Naw he just asked about his deceased daughter and Anya marrying me."

Velli was hoping that he wouldn't have to convey to his brother that Muhammad not asking about Velli only meant one thing. There was going to be some trouble.

"Listen Damu. That nigga Muhammad is a very serious dude and if he's coming around asking questions about his dead daughter that means that he is seeking payment about her death and me knowing him that only comes in blood. So, when you're moving through these streets be careful at all times you hear me? And make sure Anya checks in with you every hour on the hour by either calling or texting."

"Man fuck that nigga Muhammad. I wish he would come near my family again. I'll body his ass in broad daylight in the middle of the street about fucking with mines."

"Look Damu. It's about being cautious and safe then to be sorry later. Get a line on Muhammad and see what the hell he's up to."

"A'ight bruh. I will do that but that is your man. I just want you to know that I don't give a fuck about him."

"I never said that you had to. Since when I start putting muthafuckas before my family?"

Damu nodded his head up and down and kept driving to Velli's house. Velli rested his head back on the headrest and closed his eyes and asked Allah not to place a burden on him that he couldn't bear.

Chapter 10

Walking into his West New Haven home, Velli welcomed the sense of home. The black plush carpet buried his Timb's as he stepped into the living room where the eighty-five-inch tv hung on the wall in front of the dark beige Italian leather sofa.

"Damu, I love this place. Malaya has done her thing on decorating this place," Velli said taking in the essence of his home.

"I know right? Wait until you see the attic. Malaya never lets me go up there," Damu complained. "She says the attic is for Velli's use only. Shit bruh, I'm the one that helped her ass get all that shit up there."

Velli let out a slight chuckle.

"Yeah I go to go and check that out later."

Just then Wicket came running down the hall full speed. Wicket was a blue bloodline pit. He had a beautiful gray coat of fur. Velli saw his four-legged comrade coming at him and he dropped down to his knees and welcomed Wicket with a hug and scratched behind his ears.

"What's up big bruh," Velli said as he ruffled the fur on Wicket's big block head.

His bell cut ears made him look satanic. Malaya wasn't happy about having Wicket around when he was a puppy but once Wicket started to become obedient and show his over protectiveness for her Malaya fell in love with him. No one could control Wicket but Velli and Malaya, but Malaya was truly the dog's master. Hearing the R Kelly song, "Leg Shaken," coming form the back of the house Velli made his way to the backyard with Damu and Wicket prancing behind them. Stepping on the patio and looking into the backyard Velli saw that Malaya had arranged a small get together. This warmed Velli's heart at seeing his beautiful wife wearing the two colors that he loved to see her in, purple and pink. Malaya looked flawless in her pink and purple abayas and hijabs.

Sneaking up behind her Velli wrapped his arms around Malaya and said, "Can I have some of this sweetness with my food?" Malaya was slightly startled but quickly picked up on her husband's voice. She turned around and jumped into Velli's arms and planted kisses all over his face and lips.

"Muah, muah, muah. I missed you so much baby," Malaya said wrapping her arms around Velli's neck and squeezing him tight.

"I missed you too baby." Velli hugged his wife back with the same intensity. "Oh, baby I have something for you," Velli said releasing Malaya and pulling a small black box from his pocket and handing it to her.

"What is it baby?" Malaya questioned as she eyed the box excitedly.

"Just open the box love."

Malaya opened the box and her mouth dropped open as she stared at the pink V-cut diamond earrings that laid perfectly and peacefully in the box.

"OMG! Baby they are so beautiful!"

"Just like you are my queen," Velli said planting a kiss on Malaya's forehead.

"Veeeeeellllllliiiii," Anya screamed and ran to meet her brother-in-law with a hug.

"As Salaam Alaikum Anya."

"Wa Laikum Salaam Velli. I'm so happy that you are home. Now you can give my sister some good loving so she can relax and stop stressing."

"Anya!" Malaya gave her the evil eye and Velli busted out laughing.

"I will be sure to handle that order of good loving tonight," Velli said winking at Malaya.

Malaya blushed and put her head down. After all these years of being with Velli he still had the ability to make Malaya feel like a little schoolgirl that has a crush on a boy from school.

"Baby are you hungry?" Malaya asked trying to take herself out of the spotlight.

"Hell yeah a bruh is starving." Velli licked his lips in a sexual way while eyeing Malaya giving her the impression that he wasn't talking about food at the moment.

"Baby stop being nasty! I'm going to take my earrings in the house. I'll be right back to fix your plate."

"Okay baby that's cool."

Out of nowhere little Tiriq slammed into Velli's leg and wrapped his little arm around Velli's knee in a bear hug.

"Hey my lil nephew!" Velli picked up Tiriq and held him over his head.

Tiriq loved his uncle. If you ever saw those two interact with one another you would think that they were father and son.

"What's up Tiriq?"

Tiriq just smiled at his uncle with that big kool aid smile.

"You miss your uncle boi?"

Tiriq bopped his head up and down still smiling that smile. Velli placed Tiriq back on the ground and knelt in front of him. Anya just watched from the sidelined in awe.

"I got something for you," Velli said pulling a Spiderman watch out of his back pocket. Tiriq's eyes lit up. Spiderman was his favorite cartoon.

Putting the watch on Tiriq's small wrist Velli asked, "Do you like it?"

Tiriq looked at Velli like he was contemplating on saying something but instead he just nodded his head up and down. Velli smiled at his nephew.

"Me and Spiderman have a secret to tell you." Velli leaned in closer and put his lips inches away from Tiriq's ear. "With this watch me and Spiderman can always find you. Now go show your daddy so me and mommy can talk."

Tiriq shot off like he was running the fifty-yard dash. Standing up Velli looked at Anya.

"I hear and old friend paid you a visit the other day."

For a moment Anya just looked at Velli.

"Yeah bruh Muhammad, I mean Steve came to see me. He doesn't go by his Islamic name anymore he goes by Steve."

This wasn't good news to Velli.

"What type of demeanor did he have Anya?"

"It was really early in the morning and it was dark and cold. I couldn't really read him."

"Do you think he is a threat?"

"Naw bruh not really."

"Okay in the meantime just stay on point for anything. I mean if anything looks strange get on the phone with Damu ASAP!"

"Okay bruh I will."

"Sis, listen to me, I will protect my family by any means."

Chapter 11

Malaya stood in the full-length mirror examining herself in her new abaya. The silk champagne colored gown felt cool on her skin. Turning to the side and getting a better view, Malaya admired the Islamic gown. She felt vibrant and full of life. She couldn't believe that Velli had this gown custom designed by Vera Wang along with the hijab that she wore over her head. Sliding her pretty toes into a pair of Prada sandals and dabbing her wrists and neck with a splash of Chanel No. 5 Malaya was ready to go.

"Malaya! Come on baby girl. We are going to be late," Velli yelled from the bottom of the stairs.

"I'm coming baby. You know that you can't rush perfection," Malaya said feeling sexy and snatching her Vera Wang clutch purse and phone off the bed to make her way downstairs to meet her awaiting and impatient husband.

"Wow!" Velli's mouth fell open once he saw his wife come from upstairs. "Now I know what they mean when they make the statement drop dead gorgeous," Velli said stepping forward to place a peck on her lip gloss covered lips.

"Thanks love. You are looking sharp and handsome yourself."

"You know I try to look my best when I'm in the presence of a true Queen," Velli said feeling himself as he straightened out his suit jacket and striking a pose as if he was taking a picture for GQ magazine. Velli looked impeccable in his black Versace suit. The champagne-colored shirt he wore under the jacket matched the gown that Malaya had on. I was something about the color champagne that brought his suit to life. But what really set their outfits off was the matching his and hers Rolex watches with the champagne-colored bezel that was in the watches. "Are you ready baby girl?"

"Yes." Malaya felt good being with her husband. There was no other place she would rather be then with Velli.

Velli held the door open to his S600 Benz for Malaya. The sleek ride looked as if it was just driven off the showroom floor. The car was so clean that Malaya could see her reflection in the black car. You couldn't tell Malaya that she was anything other then a queen. Her confidence was on a thousand. Velli often made her feel that way. Sliding her round bottom into the pecan brown leather seats, Malaya thought to herself, " I just love this car."

Velli made his way into the driver's seat, started the car, and backed out of the driveway. He hit the expressway heading towards downtown Tampa from New Haven. Malaya put her back to the passenger door and watched Velli with a lascivious look in her eyes.

"Where are you taking me Velli?" Malaya asked with a smile.

"Baby just sit back and enjoy the ride," Velli said hitting the power on the luxurious machine that activated the MP3 player in the Benz. The old school jam by Rome, "I Belong to You," came blaring through the speakers and brought life to the car. Velli began singing to Malaya with the help of Rome. "Say my lady," Velli reached out to touch Malaya's knee. "Tell me what's wrong with your boyfriend. He holds the key to your heart." Malaya blissfully batted her eyes. "But he doesn't love you like I do. I only want you," Velli continued singing while he grazed his hand over her left breast. Malaya bit down on her lip. Velli kept singing to his wife. "Girl you are the love of my life baby. I belong to you, and you belong to me. I give all my love."

Malaya blushed. She never had Velli sing to her before, and he actually looked and sounded good too. This is the life and togetherness that Malaya had been yearning for. She was loving the interaction between her and her husband and had no desire for it to ever end. She knew that she had to convince Velli to forget about Stone and focus on dealing with Mango. She wanted her husband home.

Pulling up in front of Felicitous Coffee and Tea House in North Tampa off 51st street the crowd was live outside the coffee house. The Tea House was recently remodeled and everyone that was anyone made it a point to put this place on the map. Once the S600 pulled up sitting on them big, shiny rims all eyes were on the car. Malaya knew how 2Pac felt when he made that song, "All Eyes on Me," because tonight all eyes wee definitely on her and her husband. Velli opened the door for her, grabbed her hand and helped her out of the car. The women looked on with envious eyes that let Malaya know that they wished they had what she had. Looping her arm into Velli's Velli escorted her into Felicitous Coffee and Tea House.

"Baby what is this place?" Malaya asked.

"Just chill baby. You'll see," Velli said patting Malaya's hand that was gripping his arm.

Felicitous Coffee and Tea House was a beautiful establishment. It had a romantic atmosphere. The place was dimly lit but the small lights that were strung across the ceiling gave the place enough light to exude just the perfect ambiance. Malaya saw a tall sister on the stage dressed like Erykah Badu riffing off some poetic words conveying a love story about thunder and lightning over the smooth melody that the live band played in the background. Malaya became excited.

"Oh baby! Live poetry! I love poetry!"

"How could I ever forget baby girl." Velli smiled at his wife.

Finding a table in the far corner, Velli ordered a French coffee and Malaya ordered a strawberry lime tea. For the next twenty minutes Malaya and Velli snuggled close together and got lost in poet after poet as they spoke words of struggles, love, and betrayal that they encountered in their lives.

"Okay give it up for Messiha the Dar Rose," the hostess announced through the mic.

The crowd snapped their fingers in place of clapping their hands. That is how it's done in the poetry world.

"Next I want to welcome a close friend of mine and co-owner of Felicitous Coffee to the stage. He goes by Velli."

Malaya almost spit her tea out her mouth when she heard her husband's name.

"Co-owner and friend! Oh, this nigga got explaining to do," Malaya thought to herself as she watched her husband walk to the stage cool and calm with his D.C. swag. Just seeing him up on that stage made her kitty kat wet.

"Thanks Yvette," Velli said as he stepped on the stage and took the mic from the hostess. Unbuttoning his jacket Velli stared out into the audience. At that time Malaya realized that her husband was called to the stage to recite some poetry. "I dedicate this piece to my wife Malaya." Velli's voice filled the coffee house through the speakers. "It's called Smile." A soft melody began to play and Velli began to recite.

"The most fragile part of me is our strongest connection. Your kisses live in my memory with a philosophy that now offers me completion. I'm so well and it's strange to be. I'm torn by misdirection. You are my queen, my ambassador. You amplify my aspirations. So beautiful I live for you as you live for me. You make me smile. This is such a happily ever after. You travel miles and pass the finish line. We're starting on time. My tongue bears your name. If they knew where to look they would find it. You showed me I am I because you are forever so magnificent. The most amazing story I ever told. So much mote to be written. Thank you. You make me smile. I only pray

that my lips be as soft as yours. My wisdom flows so fluently from my mind. Your eyes read so truly of my spirit. Your laughter speaks the clarity of time. You are the I that I admire. You make me smile."

Velli flawlessly recited his poem without breaking eye contact from Malaya. It was like the two of them were the only two people in the room. The audience snapped their fingers loudly and praised Velli for his performance. As the tears dripped from her face the wetness dripped from between her legs too. She was ready to go and make love to her husband.

Jibril Williams

Chapter 12

Velli lay in bed with Malaya laying across his chest, both of them breathing heavily and coated in light sweat.

"Damn baby. You're the best. That hot poetry that I dropped at open mic got you on your Pinky the porn star shit."

"I better be the best." Malaya playfully punched Velli in the side. "And Pinky can't handle all this D you be slangin," Malaya said grabbing a handful of Velli's manhood. The last three days with Velli had been unbelievably great. The open mic night and the dinner on the beach in St. Pete, were both amazing. "Baby who is Yvette?" Malaya asked catching her breath.

"Oh, Yvette is Chief's wife. Me and Chief ran real heavy when I was doing my bid in Coleman Penitentiary."

"Oh, so how long have you been the owner of Felicitous Coffee and Tea House?"

Velli chuckled. "So, I guess this is what they call pillow talk huh?"

"Yeah nigga. So, spit the goods out," Malaya again playfully punched Velli in his side with her small fist.

"Well Chief hit me up a few months back while I was in D.C. and asked me for a loan to help his wife open and remodel the coffee house. I thought it was a good idea, so I loaned her the money and in return she made me co-owner. I won't take any profits from the coffee house or any money back from Yvette."

"Why not baby? It's your money that you invested in the coffee house too."

"Because I care about those that I love and that are dear to me. Chief is one of those who is dear to me," Velli said kissing Malaya on the top of her head.

Malaya didn't want to kill the vibe that her and Velli had going on at the moment and spoil their night, but she had to try to convince him to forget about D.C. and come home for good. Letting out a deep breath she just threw the question out there.

"Velli, when are you going to be finished in D.C.? I mean it's been almost three years and baby I want you home."

"I need a little bit more time. I,"

"You been telling me that same line for the last fifteen months Velli," Malaya said opening her eyes.

"I know Malaya but shit ain't just a walk in the park when you trying to take over a nigga's city."

"You mean take back your city," Malaya said lifting her head off Velli's chest and looking into his eyes. Velli couldn't maintain eye contact with his wife.

"Baby I'm trying to take care of this shit as fast as I can. So, we can get Mango off our backs."

"Fuck Stone! Fuck D.C.! Mango is our problem. He got us tied to a contract with the devil." Malaya sat up in the bed.

"I'm going to handle Stone and Mango. Let me do this shit," Velli said getting out of bed and placing his boxers and wife beater on.

"Velli I didn't go through the things that I went thought to get you of prison just to lose you right back to the streets."

"So, you want me to let that rat motherfucker Stone get away with what he done to me? Forget about the pain and hurt he caused me? Caused us?" Velli's anger mounted.

"You're the one that's hurting me right now Velli, not Stone. I can't stand to live without you any longer baby." Malaya's tears started rolling down her cheeks. "I just want you home baby. I want a family. I don't want to be a drug dealer's wife; those stories all end the same and you know it Velli."

"Malaya let me handle my business!"

"Your business is Mango, not Stone! Not the money! It's Mango. We got money Velli. We got over five million and a strong up and coming publishing company. Just come home baby please."

Velli looked into his wife's pleading eyes, turned his back, and walked out the room. Velli found himself in the attic, "The Velli Cave", is what Malaya dubbed it. His mind was in a wreck. Velli could take up any challenge he faced in the streets but when it came to his wife being unhappy he couldn't think straight.

Walking over to the small glass table that sat in the corner in the attic next to Velli's recliner he opened the cigar box and pulled out a fresh Backwoods and a stash of purp that Damu gave him. Velli wasn't really a heavy smoker but times like these when his life was stressful he'd smoke a Backwoods or two to ease his stress. Placing some heat to the Backwoods and inhaling the sweet tasting smoke, Velli sat in the recliner and let the purp escape his lungs. Thinking back on the conversation that he just had with his wife Velli knew that Malaya had all the reason to feel the way that she was feeling, and he knew that he was dragging the situation out with Stone. Now it was time to put it to rest and get back to serving his Lord and being the best Muslim that he could be. Allah had truly blessed Velli, and his family so why keep dabbing in those streets and going against his Islamic teachings? But Velli really knew why it was hard to just walk away from that Stone situation. He was never one to leave loose ends. His pride would not allow him to just let Stone betray him and not pay for it. Reaching over to the phone that sat next to recliner he hit E-Moe's number. E-Moe picked up on the third ring.

"What's up slim?" E-Moe answered the phone.

"You tell me? How shit looking? Is everything in place?"

"Yeah, we just waiting on you to touch back down in D.C."

"I'll be there in two days. When I get there we be smashing the gas you hear me?" Velli said as he let the smoke out through his nose.

"Man say no more. We waiting on you." E-Moe getting hype just thinking about what's getting ready to go down in this city.

"Alright see you soon," Velli said disconnecting the call.

Velli laid his head on the headrest of the recliner, letting the effect of the purp ease the stress from his mind.

"Betrayal is only warranted by the penalty of the death of Stone," Velli whispered.

Chapter 13

Keisha was still upset that Steve went to go see Anya the other day.

"Are you sure that you still don't have feelings for Anya?" Keisha asked poking her lips out and putting her jealousy act into play.

"Naw boo. Them feelings for Anya was buried with my daughter. Fuck Anya!"

"Okay, I really need you on board with me and Neva's plan that we put together."

"Keisha, I'm straight. I can handle this shit. Nothing comes easier to me than putting in work."

"How the fuck we know that bitch Anya is going to cough up that type of dough or do she even really have that type of money," D-Money said from across the room with Neva sitting on his lap.

"Trust me, the bitch has the bread and she'll give it up," Keisha said with an attitude. "Neva has the hardest part. Neva when shit hit the fan you gotta play your role."

"I got my end. Just make sure that I get my agreed amount once we get that money."

"Pssst, girl you going to get your money. Just play your role," Keisha said getting aggravated with her cousins.

"So, when we going to make this shit happen?" Steve asked looking at Keisha.

"As soon as you and D-Money handle y'all phase of the plan. We need Anya in as much distress as possible so when everything takes place she won't have any fight in her and she'll give that money up with no problem."

D-Money nodded his head up and down agreeing with what Keisha was saying but Steve was old school and well-seasoned. He knew that Keisha had an angle that she was playing for.

"Alright me and D-Money is going to handle the first part of the plan but once everything is in play you and Neva need to have your game tight and fulfill your end of the plan."

Steve looked at Keisha and Neva with a no bullshit look on his face.

"Our shit is together. Just make sure your emotions are in check when it's time to handle your business."

"Yeah whatever bitch!" Steve said as he made his way to the front door. "Come on D-Money we got shit to do, no time to play with pussies," Steve said smirking and exiting the front door to Keisha's apartment with D-Money stepping behind him. Keisha rolled her eyes as the front door closed behind D-Money.

"Do you think we can trust Steve and D-Money?" Neva asked jumping off the couch and getting in Keisha's face.

"Girl back the fuck outta my face," Keisha barked on her cousin. "Listen we need Steve and D-Money to do our dirty work. Once we pull this off, I got a plan to get rid of both of them fuck niggas." Keisha balled her face up thinking about what she had in store for Steve and D-Money.

"Whoa Keisha! I'm not down with killing nobody," Neva protested.

"Who said that you were going to have to kill someone?" Keisha checked her.

"Look Keisha I'm just saying killing is not for me. I'm just trying to get this money so I can start my own hair salon and get the fuck out this hell hole I'm living in," Neva reminded Keisha why she was willing to go through with the plan from the jump.

"I know cousin. You don't have to remind me," Keisha said walking away from Neva and entering the bathroom and closing the door behind her.

Opening the medicine cabinet over the sink Keisha took a bottle of eye drops and placed three drops into her left eye. She had grown accustomed to this procedure in order to keep her artificial eye feeling moist and looking real. Putting the eye drops back into the cabinet Keisha flashed back to how she lost her eye in the first place. Staring into the mirror the cute that once disfigured her face were bare visible thanks to the plastic surgeon that worked wonders on her face by removing most of the scar tissue making her beautiful again. She could never get that night she was attacked by Anya and Malaya out of her head. She recalled her facial skin being ripped by Anya and Malaya's box cutters. It was never proven that Anya and Malaya were the ones who attacked her, but her intuition was screaming Anya and Malaya's names. Tears rolled down Keisha's right cheek.

"Anya and Malaya are going to learn when a real bitch got the gun there's no ducking her wrath," Keisha said while gazing at her image in the mirror.

Chapter 14

"Everyone in place," Velli spoke to E-Moe through the blue tooth that was stuck in his ear. E-Moe, G Stack and Lil Wu sat down the street from Stone's stash house.

"Yeah slim, everything looks proper on this side of town," E-Moe spoke back through his blue tooth to Velli.

"Alright, let's get this shit done with," Velli said disconnecting the call and turning his attention to Stone's money house on 18th and Monroe Street.

Velli and E-Moe had been watching this spot for a couple of weeks now and tonight they both were going to hit Stone's coke and money houses simultaneously. Velli, Maria and Stylez got out the beat-up minivan dressed in all black from hat to boots with three yellow letters stamped across the back of their jackets and on the front of their hats. They approached the house with a swiftness while checking out their surroundings. Making their way to the front door of the house they were watching Velli gave Mario the green light.

Holding the AR-15 in his hand Mario banged on the door with the stock of his assault rifle and yelled, "F.B.I. sear warrant!"

With that Stylez kicked the door off the hinges with two strong kicks. Rushing into the house with their weapons out Stone's men were thrown off by the announcement of the F.B.I. They didn't even make an attempt to go for their guns that lay inches away from them. Once they saw that there was only three F.B.I agents they knew that something was wrong.

"Lay the fuck on the floor," Stylez yelled as he entered into the house first.

Two of the men that were in the house that were sitting on the couch dived on the floor without hesitation but the third mad was little slow, so Mario put a slug in his chest folding him over in a heap onto the floor.

"Now if you want to end up like your man over there try the slow poke game with me. Now where the money at!" Mario said through clenched teeth.

Velli loved Mario like a brother, but he was too damned trigger happy.

"It's in the back," both of the men laying on the floor said in unison.

"Where at in the back and is there anyone else in this muthafucka!" Velli asked knowing that he didn't have long before they had to get out of there. He was sure someone heard the banging and kicking on the door and if not someone certainly heard the gunshot.

"No one else is in here but us and the money is in the back in the black gym bag in the first room on the right," the guy on the floor directed Velli.

"Stylez go check that out," Velli ordered Mario to start raking money up off the living room table and to snatch the money out the money counting machine and stuff it in the bag that was lying next to the table. Velli grabbed up the guns that were laying around. "Yo Stylez, hurry the fuck up we gotta go."

Styles pressed send on his phone and stuck the phone in his pocket. Then he grabbed the bags that were on the floor slung two over his shoulder and dragged the other two bags and walked out into the living room where Velli and Mario were waiting.

Velli wasn't expecting to see Stylez carrying four bags. Velli had no idea he was coming up on so much money. He grabbed one of the bags and Mario grabbed the other. Velli was ready to leave.

"A'ight let's go," Velli ordered.

Stylez exited the house. Velli was right behind him. Looking over his shoulder Velli spoke to Mario, "You know what to do."

Mario opened fire with the assault rifle on his prisoners that laid on the floor.

*****

E-Moe had no problem gaining access to Stone's coke spot since the F.B.I trick worked like a charm. He watched Lil Wu count out the last two bricks in the duffle bag while G-Stack watched over the two old people that laid on the floor.

"Let's go slim," E-Moe instructed his two-man team.

He wasn't worried about the old lady and the man that laid tied up at his mercy. He made his way behind Lil Wu who carried half of the coke they'd gotten out the house. G-Stack led the way with the other half. Just as they were making their way to their car that was parked four houses down, a black Yukon pulled up ahead of them and two gunmen jumped out and fired on them.

Boom!

Boom!

Boom!

Their guns rung out sending E-Moe and his men scrambling. G-Stack was hit through his left cheek quickly dropping him to the ground. E-Moe and Lil Wu returned fire, lighting the quiet street up like they were at the red-carpet awards.

Blocka!

Blocka!

Blocka!

E-Moe's Ruger roared to life. Lil Wu took cover behind an SUV and fired back trying to get E-Moe some cover from the spraying bullets that were coming his way.

"Come on!" Lil Wu yelled at E-Moe hoping that he made his way to the SUV where he was shielding himself from the gunmen. The PCP had E-Moe pumped.

"Let's work nigga!" E-Moe yelled out from behind the back of a red Honda standing up and letting his Ruger rock.

Blocka!

Blocka!

Blocka!

Blocka!

Lil Wu could see that E-Moe was in a zone. E-Moe tried to make his way over to where G-Stack was and retrieve the bag with the coke in it, but the gunmen weren't letting up. Wu dropped one of the gunmen leaving him sprawled out next to the passenger side of the truck that he got out of. Hearing sirens in the distance all shooters knew that it was a matter of time before they were surrounded by the Metropolitan Police. The remaining gunman sent more shots Wu's way before making his way back behind the driver's seat of the truck but not before a bullet bounced off the sidewalk and hit Wu in the shin sending him to the concrete in pain.

E-Moe fresh out of bullets tucked his gun and ran to where G-Stack laid dead to get his gun that was lying next to him. The gunman zipped away in truck and E-Moe squeezed off two shots dropping the shooter's back window.

Running over to Lil Wu E-Moe asked, "Can you get up Slim?"

"Naw Slim. You got to get me to the car."

The sirens could still be heard in the background getting closer. E-Moe snatched up Lil Wu by the arms with the bag of coke still strapped to his shoulder. He rushed Lil Wu to the waiting car pushing him in the back seat hopping behind the wheel. He pulled before the police could get there leaving G-

Stack laying dead on the sidewalk next to twenty bricks of coke.

Chapter 15

Damu passed the Backwoods to his partner, Biggz, that sat in the passenger seat as they cruised down Nebraska Avenue heading to Robert's projects.

"Damn Damu, this weed is some straight fire!" Biggz said as he deeply inhaled the weed.

"Yeah I got that shit right off the west coast," Damu said adjusting the volume of the music in the Range Rover.

Damu met Biggz through his wife Anya a few years ago when she and Malaya used to sell drugs for Mike. Biggz was Mike's right hand man, but once Velli and Damu killed his supplier Mike, Anya basically turned Mike's major buyers over to Damu. Damu really played to the background and let Biggz have the spotlight as the mad in the streets of Tampa. Only a handful of people really knew who Damu was.

"Man, you should get a couple of pounds of this shit and let me flood Tampa with this shit," Biggz said taking another pull on the Backwoods and passing it back to Damu.

"Shit Biggz. I see that two great minds think alike. I was just thinking the same thing the other day," Damu said blowing out smoke through his nose.

Driving by Seminole Elementary and stopping at the light at the intersection Damu was in a zone, bobbing his head up and down listening to Rick Ross talk that talk in his song, "Pirates." He was so into the music that he never saw the green Caddie coming up on his rear until it was too late, and it rammed into the back of his truck. Hearing and feeling the crunch of his bumper knocked the Backwoods out of his hand.

"What the fuck!" Biggz yelled turning around trying to see what was going on behind him.

Damu threw the truck into park and looked through his rearview mirror. He saw that the caddie behind him and was occupied by two people with their hats pulled low over their faces. Seeing the green Caddie ease back off of his bumper but never exiting their car Damu felt shit wasn't right. Before he could react Biggz opened his door and started to get out the truck.

"Hold up Biggz!" Damu shouted grabbing his gun from between the seat and got out the truck.

"Man, what fuc." That was all Biggz got out his mouth before the doors on the Caddie flew open and the two occupants got out their guns.

Pow!

Pow!

Pow!

Boom!

Boom!

Boom!

Biggz made a run for the sidewalk keeping his head low as he ran. Damu banged back at the killers.

Blocka!

Blocka!

Trying to hit one of the men that was shooting at him but too many shots were fired his way. Catching a bullet in the shoulder Damu fell to the ground and his gun slid from his hand into the street. Damu crawled to the front of his truck trying to get away from the shooters. Damu tried to push himself up on his feet by using the front bumper of the truck, but he fell back to the ground. Damu knew this was the end for him.

He could hear footsteps running towards him and he just laid there looking up at the midnight sky. Moments later, a figure stood over him. Damu was looking at the barrel of a black handgun. The man with the gun was looking down at Damu. Damu couldn't see his face totally because his hat was still pulled down over his face. The gunman smiled and squeezed the trigger, but nothing happened. The gun was jammed. The roar of Biggz's .44 caliber, boom, boom, boom, boom, made the man standing over Damu flinch and retreat back to the waiting green Caddie with the other shooter and retreat with their lives.

Biggz looked down at Damu with the large cannon gripped tight in his hand.

"You a'ight my nigga?" Biggz questioned.

"I've been hit Biggz," Damu said before he passed out from pain.

*****

"Damn!" Steve said, banging his hand on the steering wheel of the stolen Caddie.

D-Money checked his passenger mirror to see if the police or Damu and Biggz were behind them.

"Man calm down and drive," D-Money said placing his head on the headrest trying to get his heart rate under control. "We'll get another chance if he isn't dead already."

"D-Money that nigga ain't dead," Steve yelled.

"We don't know that yet. I did hit him when he tried to get up and he fell back down and just laid there."

"Man, that don't mean shit." Steve was mad that his gun jammed and before he could unjam it that nigga Biggz came from out of nowhere with that cannon. He thought Biggz ran off and left Damu to die but Biggz came back busting at him. He could still feel the bullets of Biggz's gun wheezing past his head.

"Let's get rid of the car and make it back to Keisha's house," D-Money said as Steve turned off Nebraska Avenue.

Jibril Williams

Chapter 16

Malaya and Anya got the call from Biggz thirty minutes ago that Damu had been shot. Biggz dropped him off at Mercy General and got ghost. He couldn't stick around knowing that the police would be there asking questions that he couldn't answer with two burners on him and warrants on his head.

"This shit can't be happening!" Anya cried out as she pounded her fists into thighs. Malaya pushed the Lexus up to 85 mph heading to the hospital.

"It's going to be alright. Anya just calm down," Malaya said trying to comfort her best friend and sister in faith. "Allah will protect him."

"Malaya this can't be happening to me, not to my husband," Anya wiped her runny nose with the sleeve of her shirt.

"Damu is a warrior, lust just like my husband. He will pull through this," Malaya said with great conviction deep down inside she was praying and hoping that she was right about Damu pulling through this situation.

Biggz didn't give many details on where Damu was shot at or who shot him He was just rambling, but they did understand him to say that they were in a shootout. Damu got shot in the gun battle and blacked out from his injury. Malaya and Anya assumed the worst.

Anya called Malaya and Neva in a panic giving them the news of Damu being shot. Neva was watching Tiriq while Anya went to see about Damu. Anya didn't want Tiriq to be at the hospital not knowing if Damu was going to make it or not. Pulling into Tampa General Anya and Malaya wasted no time as they both bolted out of the car and ran towards the entrance of the hospital. They made their way to the nurses' station. Anya was still crying, and she couldn't bring herself to say Damu's name. Grabbing Anya's hand Malaya spoke for her sister.

"Excuse me," Malaya said interrupting the pretty blonde nurse that was engrossed in paperwork behind the nurses' station.

"How may I help you?" the nurse replied.

"Yes my brother Brandon Williams was brought in here tonight for gunshot wounds."

The nurse struck a few keys on the computer's keyboard.

"Oh, here he is. He just came out of surgery."

Hearing this drove Anya to her knees as if someone sucker punched her in the stomach. Malaya knelt down to console her.

"Anya pull it together," Malaya began to cry.

"If you two would please have a seat over there in the waiting area I will go and get the doctor so he can speak with you."

Malaya nodded her head acknowledging the nurse's request. Anya and Malaya sat in the waiting room for about twenty-five minutes before a short white bald-headed doctor came into waiting area.

"Mrs. Williams!"

"Yes!" Anya jumped from her seat.

"Hi, I'm Dr. Shams. I performed the surgery on your brother."

"No, I'm his wife," Anya corrected.

"Oh okay. I'm sorry. I performed the surgery on your husband." Dr. Sham extended his hand to Anya.

"Is he alright?" Anya pleaded.

"Of course, he will be. He just needs plenty of rest. He was shot in the left shoulder. The bullet ended up getting lodged behind his collarbone. I removed it and he will be fine." The doctor reassured Anya.

"All praises are due to Allah," Anya whispered under breath. "When can I see him?"

"Tomorrow. He just came out of surgery, and he is still a bit groggy. He needs to get some rest but tomorrow you can see him and if all is well he'll be home in three to four days." Hearing this made Anya smile.

Malaya had been calling Velli like crazy trying to relay the news about his brother getting shot. She started to worry.

"Come on baby. Please call me back. I need to hear your voice. Let me know that you are okay," Malaya whispered to herself as she pulled out her phone to text her husband again.

Chapter 17

Velli paced back and forth in the two-bedroom apartment on Morton Street N.W. better known in the city of D.C. as six-forty.

"What the fuck happened E-Moe?" Velli said still walking the floor.

"Slim them niggas just came from out of nowhere, busting and shit. They definitely were Stone's men because I recognized Stone's little brother, Mookie. They must have been on the way to the stash house to pick some shit up because the old bitch and man had like three joints sitting by the front door in the living room.

"Damn!" Velli shouted out in anger. "I wanted this shit to go smoothly," Velli said as he took a seat in the chair next to where the bag of coke E-Moe and his men robbed Stone for was sitting. Placing his head in his hands Velli asked, "Do you think the nigga Mookie recognized you E-Moe?"

"Slim I don't know but if I recognized Mookie then most likely he knew who the fuck I was. Velli that's water under the bridge. We made our move so fuck Stone bitch ass." E-Moe voiced his opinions while he cleaned his Glock 40.

"I'm with you on that one," Mario said puffing on a blunt full of PCP. The chemicals from the PCP had Mario and E-Moe full of nothing but homicidal thoughts running through their minds as they were mourning the loss of their nigga G-Stack.

"How much money we came off with?" Mario asked Velli.

"A little over $200,000 in small bills."

"Daaaaamn! I didn't think that that nigga was bringing in that type of money." Stylez never said anything just taking in everything he was hearing.

"I think that we should give G-Stack's mother his share of the money," E-Moe said standing and stretching his legs.

"I think that's some righteous shit to do." Mario agreed with E-Moe.

"We got twenty bricks from the stash house."

E-Moe walked over and grabbed the bag that was sitting next to Velli's feet. Dumping the work on the floor Velli couldn't believe what he was seeing. E-Moe saw the look on his partner's face.

"Damn Slim you act like you ain't never seen twenty bricks at one time before," E-Moe said with a smirk.

Velli was floored.

"This couldn't be right," he thought to himself.

"Velli what the fuck is up?" E-Moe questioned.

"Man, them bricks came from our supplier. Them joints came from Mango."

"Man get the fuck outta here. You bullshitting Slim," Mario said from the couch.

"They have the same Texas star stamp on the package. Mango is the only one that uses the Texas star champ." Then the realization hit Velli like a ton of bricks. "That fat muthafucka has been playing me the whole time," Velli said out loud. "He's supplying Stone too." Velli jumped out the chair. "Look I got to go take care of some shit. Start moving the work and go visit G-Stack's mother and take her his half of the money and give her my cut too. And somebody go by the hospital and check up on Lil Wu," Velli said as he walked to the door. "I want everyone on point and strapped."

Giving his men their orders Velli made his way to his car and grabbed his phone off his hip. He had to call Damu and give him the news that he had just discovered. Realizing his phone was off Velli hit the power button and saw that he had thirty missed calls and texts. He opened the last text from

Malaya. His hands shook as he read the text. *Damu has been shot. Call home ASAP!*

Jibril Williams

Chapter 18

Stone listened to his little brother unveil the events of the last night to him. Stone listened with a cold heart and murderous mind. He hadn't been that furious since that day Velli handed over their coke connect to Damu along with the keys to the city.

"Man fuck!" Stone screamed. "And you couldn't stop them niggas from getting away with my product?"

"Naw Stone. We had a big fucking shoot out in the middle of southeast," Mookie said getting mad and feeling like Stone only gave a fuck about the drugs and money that he lost. "My man Trey got smashed last night protecting your shit. I barely escaped with my life."

Ignoring Mookie Stone stroked his goatee.

"So, who is this nigga that sent you the text saying that my spot was being robbed?"

"It's a nigga that I did some time with over the D.C. jail last year when I went in for that gun charge. I seen the nigga last month ant H2O night club. We traded information but I really don't know him like that," Mookie said looking at his brother.

"So how the fuck this nigga know that my shit was getting robbed?"

"I don't know Stone. I been calling and texting his nigga all morning, but I haven't gotten and answer."

"Alright when you get a hold of the chump nigga set up a meeting with him. I need to talk to him." Stone looked at Mookie with a look that told a lie and Mookie knew that his brother was going to kill dude.

"Are you sure that it was Velli and E-Moe that you had a shootout with?"

"Yeah Stone, I'm sure that it was them. I can recognize E-Moe's lanky ass from anywhere." Mookie knew that he'd never seen Velli last night at the shootout, but he knew that E-Moe was Velli's man and if E-Moe was there then Velli sent him. Stone had heard enough, and he had some calls to make.

"Alright Mookie. I'll holla at you later. I have some shit to do."

"A'ight bro. You be safe through your travels."

"Likewise," Stone replied.

Mookie gave his brother a pound on his hand and left the house. Stone grabbed the phone that sat next to him on the same couch that he fucked Mookie's baby mama on just a few weeks ago. He hit the button on speed dial placing the phone to his ear and waiting for the phone to ring on the other end. The phone rang five times before a familiar voice answered the phone.

"Rude boi!" the Jamaican accent hit Stone's ear.

"I need to hire you and your brothers' company to kill a few bugs that have been bugging me," Stone said.

"Me need to know how big dem roaches be rude boi."

"Let's just say $50,000 for the whole job. I need this job done ASAP though!"

"Dem roached bring mad problems for de Stoney huh rude boi?"

"Yeah you can say that," Stone said rubbing his hand over his wavy hair. "You remember the nigga Velli, and E-Moe I was telling you about a few months ago?"

"Me member Stoney and me and me brethren are on it rude boi so no sweatin it. Jus make sure me money be right you know?"

With that the phone went dead. Stone took a deep breath. He felt better knowing that them crazy ass Jamaican killers, Nebo and Pebo, were on the hunt for Velli and E-Moe. Stone didn't have to wait for five rings like he did for the last call. This caller picked up on the first ring when Stone called.

"Hola mi amigo!"

"Yo Mango, we need to talk I have a problem."

Chapter 19

Anya walked into Damu's hospital room and seeing her husband laying there with IV's running from his arms and the heart monitor clipped to his finger brought mist to her eyes. Seeing the blood-stained bandage covering his left shoulder was too much for her. She rushed to Damu's bedside and gently touched his face. Damu and Tiriq were her life. She couldn't imagine living without either of them. When she lost her daughter almost three years ago Damu came into her life like a knight in shining armor and he had never left her side. Tears really started pouring down her face reflecting on the thoughts of her past. She placed a kiss on Damu's forehead.

"I love you baby," Damu stirred in his bed.

"I love you back," Damu said opening his eyes.

Upon hearing her husband's voice and seeing his eyes open sent Anya's tears into overdrive. She forgot that he just had surgery and wrapped her arms around his neck and squeezed him tight.

"OMG baby are you okay?!" Anya cried.

"Ouch, ouch, ouch! Baby please!" Damu cried out.

Realizing her affections were hurting Damu she released her grip and settled for placing kisses on his face.

"I'm sorry baby. I didn't mean to hurt you," Anya said between kisses. "Baby I thought I lost you."

"It's going to take more than one bullet to put me down for the count," Damu sounded weak, but he wanted to seem strong for his wife. "I'm alright baby. I'm not punching out on you no time soon," Anya looked at her husband with eyes of sorrow.

"Damn I want you out them streets. I want you home with me and Tiriq."

"Come on baby. You going to let a little scare take me out the game? There's money to be made out there."

"We got money Damu. We're not hurting for nothing. Let's start living baby."

"What about Mango?"

"We can handle him just like we handled Redz," Anya pleaded.

"We just can't roll up on Mango like that. Mango is a boss. You can't just kill a man of that status and just walk away without repercussions," Damu said hitting the button on his bed to bring him up to a sitting position.

"If we execute the right plan it can be done." Damu loved when his wife went into her gangsta mode. "Baby, Tiriq needs his father." Damu looked away from Anya. She knew how much Damu loved his son and she just used Tiriq to get to Damu and to get what she wanted.

Damu looked back at his wife.

"I'm going to make it happen baby but not until I'm sure we can kill Mango and get away with it. We can't rush this."

"Okay baby," Anya said thankful that she didn't have to argue with her husband. "The doctor said you can go home tomorrow once they can see no infection has set in your wound."

"I can't wait. I'm ready to be home. Where's Biggz?" Damu said switching the subject.

He tole Anya how Biggz saved his life and if it wasn't for him he wouldn't be there talking to her. Anya just listened to Damu's story on the attempt on his life. Anya thanked Allah that Biggz was there last night.

Chapter 20

Ten days later...

"Yeah, bruh, I'm feeling just fine," Damu said talking to Velli on the phone. "My shoulder is a little stiff but other than that I'm still the same ole G," Damu laughed.

"Okay slim I hear ya."

"Bruh you know that your sister-in-law has been in my ear about getting out the game."

"Damn Malaya must have gotten to Anya because she had been singing that same damn song."

"Shit Velli we can't blame them. We supposed to be living life somewhere eating lobsters and shrimp, running butt naked on somebody's island but we got this fat bean and rice eating muthafucka putting the long-range press game down on us. It's about time we go ahead and put that plan together and bake that nigga Mango a cake."

'I'll start putting that into play once I handle this problem here in D.C. It's about time that I pay Stone a visit face to face and put an end to all this madness. I got a line on some bitch that this nigga Stone be fucking."

"A'ight but don't leave room for error Velli," Damu said.

"Oh, I won't but switching gears for a minute bruh. Whatchu think about them niggas trying to slump you?"

"Velli I'm not gonna lie them niggas was straight gunning for a nigga slim."

"Oh yeah?"

"When Biggz ran them niggas didn't even shoot his way. They were only busting at me."

"So, you have no clue who they were?"

"Naw slim. I got Biggz out there with his ear to the streets though."

"You don't think Biggz had anything to do with it?"

"I can't say that he did bruh. He could have just let them niggas kill me. I mean the nigga was standing over me with a gun in his hand and everything until Biggz started busting his gun."

"Have you ruled out Muhammad, Anya's ex-husband?"

"I been thinking along them lines but there's nothing to confirm it though bruh."

"A'ight just keep your eyes open and stay safe. I love you bruh."

"The feelings are the same," Damu said. "Before I go have you talked to Malaya?"

"Yeah she's jive mad at me for not answering my phone the night you got shot. She said I had her worried."

"Well welcome to the world of being a husband," Damu said laughing and disconnected the call.

Chapter 21

Steve watched the smoke drift from the burning cigarette that was resting in between his fingers. His mind was in another world. He couldn't believe that he had a chance to kill Damu and failed because his gun jammed. He knew it would be a cold day in hell before he would get another chance like that to kill Damu. But the next opportunity that he got he vowed to himself he wouldn't miss. Taking a pull from the cigarette and letting the smoke seep from his nose, Steve ran his hand over his Caesar cut.

"Fuck!" he wished that he could have killed Damu.

"There's no need to sit there with your lip all poked out looking like a sad puppy," Keisha said entering the bedroom with nothing on but a black pair of boy shorts. Walking over to her dresser grabbing a bottle of lotion and working the lotion into her skin Steve watched with a lustful eye.

"We going to have to move on to the second part of the plan," Keisha said sliding the pink booty shorts over her Kenya Moore shaped ass. "Being as though you don't know how to kill anybody," Keisha added insult to Steve's wounded morale.

"Bitch! Didn't I tell you that the fucking gun jammed on me?"

"Yeah whatever," Keisha said rolling her eyes at Steve for calling her a bitch.

Keisha pulled the tight fitted wife beater over her head. The top showed no mystery as to whether or not Keisha had a bra on or not. Her nipples budded up like it was a cold winter night.

"So, when we going to get ready to make that next move," Steve said walking up behind Keisha as she placed her Brazilian weave in a tight ponytail.

"When I say that we are ready." She ignored Steve's presence behind her and placed her Mack lip gloss on. Keisha could feel Steve's manhood against her butt. "This nigga is so pressed," she thought to herself.

"When you going to give me some of this?" Steve wrapped his arms around the front of Keisha and cupped her vicious camel toe in the palm of his hand.

"When shit starts going right for us, then you can get some loving," Keisha said spinning out of Steve's arms and walking over to the bed to grab her Chanel purse and cell phone.

"Where the fuck you think you going?" Steve asked.

"For me to know and for you to find out," Keisha said as she smirked and exited the bedroom.

*****

"Neva, could you have the editing work done by the end of the day?" Anya asked from the doorway of Neva's office.

"Yeah sure. You'll have it way before the end of the day," Neva said logging off her computer and getting ready for her lunch break. "I'm heading out for lunch. Do you want me to bring you back something?"

"Naw girl, I'm good. Thanks anyway."

"What about you Tiriq? You want a cookie?" Tiriq nodded his head up and down as he stood behind his mother in the doorway.

"Girl he doesn't need anything," Anya tried to interject.

"No, it's okay Anya. I got him. I'll see you in an hour." Neva grabbed her purse and headed to the front door of BAM Publications.

Working for Anya and Malaya wasn't actually bad. Neva actually liked her job. If it wasn't for Keisha's influence over he she would probably be looking into a career at BAM

Publications. But Neva was like everyone else in the world. She wanted her own shit point blank and would go to any distance to get it. Stepping out of BAM Publications' office building onto the sidewalk of downtown Tampa the sun hit her in the eyes making her throw on her Prada shades.

Neva strutted down the street heading to her favorite lunch spot. The sun dress clung to her curves revealing her hourglass shape. Neva was a bombshell standing 5'7 and rocking a blonde Mohawk with grey eyes. Her mother was black, but her father was mixed with so many different nationalities that she didn't really know what her DNA consisted of. She inherited her grey eyes from her father, but she definitely obtained everything else from her mother. Neva had a small waist and a K. Michelle ass with small titties, but she was every man's dream. As Neva walked down the street she got a few honks from cars driving by but what really got Neva was how she would catch women staring at her with a lustful stare as she walked down the street.

"I'm a bad muthafucka," she thought to herself. As she walked into Chili's, Neva's stomach growled with no time placing her order.

"Yes, may I have the seafood platter with a small Caesar salad," Neva said to the woman who was behind the counter.

"And what would you like to drink ma'am?"

"Hmmmmm, I'll have iced tea please."

"Okay that will be $12.56 please."

"I got that," a voice behind Neva chimed in as an arm reached around her to hand the cashier a $20 bill.

When Neva turned around to thank the generous man who just bought her lunch, Neva's jaw dropped larger than the Tampa Sun rail tunnel and remained that way for what seemed like an eternity. Backing up against the counter she stared into the eyes of Mike.

Chapter 22

Velli, E-Moe and Stylez cruised down Georgia Avenue. They pulled up into the parking lot of McDonald's on the back side of Howard University.

"Stylez go through the drive thru slim," E-Moe said from the back seat of the black on black 745 BMW.

"Naw E-Moe, it's some young pussy that works in the McDonald's that's on my dick. I'm trying to holla real quick and plus you know once I spit this hot game in her ear we'll be getting our food for free."

"Nigga! You ain't got no game Bama ass nigga!" E-Moe said giving Stylez a hard time.

Velli just shook his head at his comrades from the passenger seat. Getting out the car Velli's sixth sense went off. Something just didn't feel right. He scanned the McDonald's parking lot. He saw a tall Jamaican dude standing by the McDonald's entrance jiggling a cup with some change in it. The Jamaican man asked everyone for some spare change as they walked in and out of the establishment. Velli could feel that something was odd about this picture because he couldn't see the man's eyes as they were blocked by a pair of dark shades. E-Moe and Stylez walked past the dread head as if he wasn't even there. Velli got a closer look as he prepared to enter the restaurant. The dread head was too clean to be a panhandler and the big gold chain around his neck that he tried to conceal under his shirt was a dead giveaway.

"Yo me brethren, spare me some change mon."

Sorry slim. Fresh outta change," Velli said. "Fake ass con man," Velli whispered to himself as he pushed past the man.

Velli glanced over his shoulder to see another dread head get out of a black van on the other side of the parking lot. He caught up with Stylez and E-Moe. Styles was already laying his game down to the young girl that worked at McDonald's counter.

"So, what time you getting off because you know a nigga trying to come through and holla at you," Stylez said licking his lips.

"I'll be getting off around 8:00pm tonight. You really gonna come and pick me up this time because the last time you never showed up when you were supposed to pick me up from work," the young girl said prancing back and forth on her feet and biting down on her bottom lip indicating that she was down with giving Stylez some of her lovin'.

"I might be busy around that time but give a nigga a call once you get home and cleaned up. You know I don't want that thang smelling like French fries and number three's when I get there," Stylez said laughing.

"Whatever!" the girl said rolling her eyes. "You said that the last time, but I called you and you never returned my call."

"Lil mama I just got caught up that night but give me a chance to make it up to you."

"You promise Stylez?"

"I promise baby. Now give me and my men some food so we can get out of here," Stylez said blowing the young girl a kiss.

Velli was getting impatient waiting and watching Stylez's weak ass game. He hated when older dudes ran game on young girls that didn't know any better. That young girl had a slamming body and a set of lips that could probably massage a nigga's dick into a coma, but Velli wouldn't fuck with her, she was barely legal. Besides, he didn't cheat on his wife. Velli got out of line with Stylez and E-Moe and got into the next line and placed his order with the fat chick that was behind the counter trying to look cute.

"Yeah let me get a number five and an orange soda and an apple pie."

"Will that be all sir?"

"Yeah that will be all."

"Okay that will be $10.95."

Velli handed the girl a $50 bill.

"Keep the change."

The girl couldn't believe her eyes.

"Thank you so much sir! Your order will be right up."

Velli scanned the McDonald's. There weren't too many people occupying the spot. He could no longer see the fake Jamaica that was posted up outside the front door.

"Here you go sir, enjoy," the heavy cashier said handing Velli his order behind the counter.

"Thanks. Have a good one," Velli said and walked away from the counter. E-Moe and Styles were pulling away from the counter where the young girl stood.

"Man, shawty hooked us up," E-Moe said checking the contents in his bad as they walked out of the McDonald's.

"Aye slim. I got something to say to the broad right quick," Stylez said turning around and heading back into the restaurant.

Velli and E-Moe headed to the car. Velli saw the dread head that was standing outside two cars down from where they were parked. Velli saw something he missed the first time. The dread head had an earpiece hanging from his ear.

"Hold up E-Moe."

Velli reached out and grabbed E-Moe's arm. Just then the other dread head Velli saw earlier stepped from the side of Stylez's BMW carrying a 12-gauge shot gun.

Boom!

Boom!

Boom!

The gauge rocked the parking lot. Velli dropped his bag and sprinted away from the dread head that was bringing war in the parking lot. He drew his gun and dipped in between two cars with E-Moe right behind him.

"What the fuck slim!" E-Moe said breathing hard and pulling the chrome .45 off his hip. "Where the fuck is Stylez? I know he heard them shots!"

Velli peeped under the car that he was hiding behind to see if he could see his assassin coming his was coming his way and sure enough there were two sets of legs coming their way.

"E-Moe let's move. They coming slim!" Velli yelled standing up and releasing shots from his Glock.

Blocka!

Blocka!

Blocka!

Boom!

Boom!

Boom!

The .45 E-Moe carried let its presence be known. The dread heads returned fire, but their shot guns were no match for the automatic weapons that Velli and E-Moe had. Ducking back down behind the car the dreads used that time to retreat. Hearing wheels squealing, Velli peeked back over the trunk of the car and was happy to see the dreads were taking off in the van.

"E-Moe go get that nigga Stylez and let's get the fuck outta here," Velli said still clutching his Glock.

E-Moe ran into the McDonald's yelling for Stylez, but he was nowhere to be found.

Chapter 23

Damu listened intensely as his brother Velli relayed the events of him almost being killed yesterday.

"Damn bruh what the fuck is going on? A muthafucka tried to off my ass a few weeks ago and yesterday two Jamaicans tried to murk you," Damu said sitting on the couch watching his son Tiriq play with his toys on the floor.

"I know slim. Shit is crazy," Velli confirmed how Damu was feeling.

"So, you think that it as Stone behind the hit?"

"Man, I believe it was Stone and Mango behind that move."

"Mango too?! But why would Mango want to kill you bruh? We been doing good business with that clown."

"I feel you Damu but why the fuck this fat Spanish fucka supplying Stone behind our backs?"

"That's a mystery we both got to solve Velli."

"Oh, I plan on finding out," Velli said.

"Any word on that chump nigga Stylez?"

"Naw me or E-Moe haven't heard shit about that scary ass nigga, but something isn't right with Stylez."

"Maybe he had something to do with the hit. Maybe he set the whole thing up," Damu said on the other end of the phone.

Velli sat up in the chair and took a deep breath.

"I feel like you feel Damu. That is what my instincts tell me, but we will talk more about this later," Velli said hanging up the phone.

*****

Neva sat at the kitchen table sipping tea with her mind in a trance thinking about her encounter with Mike the other day. She couldn't believe how things were playing out for her.

"Neva! Neva!" Keisha yelled drawing Neva from her thoughts and making her jump. "What the fuck is wrong with you?" Keisha said standing in the doorway of the kitchen.

"Oh, oh, nothing. I'm good Keisha."

"Well, you sitting there like you in love or something. I hope that you not falling for the dumb fuck nigga, D-Money."

"Cuz you know that I'm not even into D-Money so stop playing," Neva said rolling her eyes.

"Well, I hope that you are ready to handle that business tomorrow and don't get cold feet at the last minute. I need your shit tight," Keisha said eyeing Neva.

"Don't worry about tomorrow. I got my end under control. Just worry about yours," Neva said placing her cup in the sink and leaving the kitchen.

Chapter 24

"Slim, I'm telling you them dumb ass Jamaicans was faking like shit with bullshit guns. Don't nobody be using shotguns no more. Niggas running the streets with thirty round clips on their sides not a five-shot pump," Stylez said biting down on a chicken wing that he just purchased from KFC. Mookie slapped the wing out of Stylez's mouth with lightning speed.

"Listen Stylez, all the fuck you had to go do was drive the fucking car through the drive thru like we planned."

Stylez sat there shocked that Mookie had the nuts to slap the wing out his mouth.

"Man, I don't know them dreads. What if one of the muthafuckas would have me by accident?" Let the truth be told Stylez was scared that Stone and Mookie was going to have him killed anyway.

"Man fuck all that. We need you to set up another move so we can get another change to smash this nigga Velli."

"Man, I don't know about that. I haven't been around Velli or E-Moe since the shooting."

"What?! You mean to tell me that your bitch ass hadn't been to holla at Velli and them since the shooting? You should have shown your face. Now they might put two and two together and think that you put the whole move together," Mookie said shaking his head at Stylez's dumb ass.

"I'm going to call Velli and see how he is talking."

"Yeah you do that. Don't forget that Stone still wanna meet with you."

Stylez knew this was where the double cross would come into play.

"A'ight. Let me first see if I can get back on Velli's team so when I meet with your brother I can give him some info on Velli's next move."

"Well make that happen cuz I can't keep my brother waiting for ling," Mookie said as he got up from the table at KFC where he and Stylez were sitting. "Oh, let me ask you something. How did you know that my brother's spot was getting robbed?" Mookie looked Stylez straight in the eyes looking for any sign that he was lying.

"That nigga G-Stack told me the night he was going on the move with Velli and E-Moe," Stylez said with a straight face.

*****

"Damn shorty you geekin like shit and you getting on my last nerve," Mario said to the stripper that he just left the hotel with. She was riding in the passenger seat of his new white BMW truck.

"Mario, stop being petty. I'm just hungry. Look there's a KFC right there. Just pull over so I can get something to eat," the stripper begged as she slid over and stuck her tongue in his ear and sucked his ear lobe.

Mario couldn't resist the stripper's tongue game and he knew that her head was the truth. He was definitely going to sample it again before he dropped her back off at the club. Whipping the pretty truck into the KFC parking lot, Mario handed the stripper a crispy $20 bill.

"Don't be long. I got shit to do."

"Boi I won't!" the stripper said umping out the car and strutting across the parking lot heading towards KFC.

Mario seen two dudes coming out the KFC. His homicidal mind clicked on like a light switch. Stylez and Mookie walked out the KFC gave each other some dap and went their separate ways. Mario grabbed his cell phone and called E-Moe. E-Moe who chillin with Velli picked up on the second ring.

"Hello?"
"E-Moe this is Mario. Slim, you ain't gon believe this…"

Chapter 25

Neva's stomach did butterflies, and she couldn't get her nerves under control.

"Come on Neva. Pull yourself together," she attempted to coach herself.

Grabbing her laptop and French vanilla coffee, she exited the car. The small parking lot that held BAM Productions seemed larger then normal as Neva made her way to her workplace. Walking into the office building she was greeted by the office secretary.

"Good morning Neva."

"Good morning Pam," Neva replied and headed straight to her office which was located at the back of BAM Publications office building.

Unlocking her office door tossing her laptop on her desk and placing the coffee on the right-hand side of her desk she began her work for the day. Her mind couldn't stay focused. Her thoughts were on the task at hand, but her heart was with Mike.

"Oh God ain't he a helluva man!" Neva spoke to herself.

"Who's a helluva man?" Malaya said entering Neva's office.

"Oh, nobody Malaya."

"That nobody got you talking like that? Speaking to yourself and everything?" Malaya said smiling at Neva.

"Hummm, it's nobody. Nobody you would know anyway. But when things get real juicy and hot between us, I'll let you know something because I'm going to need a few days off, if you know what I mean," Neva said winking her eye and smiling back at Malaya.

"Alright then girl. Are you finished editing the manuscript for Incarcerated Hearts yet?"

"Yes I did. I already emailed it to you soon as I got in this morning."

"Okay let me go check my emails pull the manuscript and start working on the cover for the book. Oh, that reminds me, I still have it do a cover for the love story, Blind Love."

"The title sounds interesting. Awww who is coming to pay me a visit this morning," Neva said to Tiriq peeking around the corner of her office door. Little Tiriq emerged fully in Neva's doorway and into Neva's office with a big ole Kool-Aid smile on his face.

"Hey Tiriq," Malaya greeted her nephew.

*****

"Man, I'm positive that it was that nigga Stylez with Mookie," Mario said taking a pull of his Newport.

"That must be how Mookie know we was robbing the stash house," E-Moe said twiddling the Rambo style knife back and forth in his hand and nodding at Velli. "This nigga is playing both sides of the fence and that bitch nigga knows all about our operation," E-Moe replied to Mookie on the phone.

"He does know a lot about our shit, but he doesn't know that we know that he is playing the ends against the middle. We mush use that to our advantage and make it work for us," Velli said walking to the window with his hands behind his back. The small apartment on Morton Street felt cramped. "We need to find the nigga Stylez." Velli pressed his face against the cool window.

E-Moe interrupted their conversation. To his surprise it was Stylez calling.

*****

Neva's hands were sweating nonstop.

"Okay, breathe Neva breathe," Neva said to herself. She reached for her phone and dialed a few numbers. The phone was picked up on the first ring.

"Yeah," the man answered the hone on the other end.

"I'm getting ready to go on my break. Where are you?"

"I'm sitting in the parking lot right next to your window."

"Are you ready?" Neva whispered.

"Let's do it."

"Alright when you see my window open come to the window," Neva disconnected the call.]

Neva walked into the hallway where Tiriq was playing with his action figures.

"Psst, psst, psst!" Neva signaled to Tiriq.

Little Tiriq stopped playing to see where the noise was coming from. He saw Neva beckoning him to come into her office. Neva was one of his favorite people that worked at his mother's job. Neva always had dome sweets for him, so he took off running towards her office. As soon as he made it to Neva's office something was thrown over his head and he was picked up.

Neva rushed Tiriq to the open window and tended him to the male figure. That male figure disappeared quickly from the window and threw Tiriq in the car where another man was waiting, and they pulled off. Neva immediately closed her window and grabbed her phone and keys off the desk. She quietly walked down the hall and unlocked the back door to the office building and left the door ajar. Neva then made her way up the hall past the secretary.

"Pam, I'm going to lunch if anybody asks."

"Okay Neva."

Neva walked out the office building threw her shades on and started strutting towards her favorite eatery. Dialing a number on her phone the man picked up on the second ring.

"Hey baby girl."

"Hey Mike." Neva melted in her panties. "It's done."

Chapter 26

"Man, I don't see this nigga out here E-Moe," Velli said checking his surroundings while they sat in the middle of the block of 14th and Park Road Northwest.

This used to be Velli and E-Moe's old stomping grounds before Velli went to prison eleven years ago. Things really had changed for the neighborhood. The district remodeled the neighborhood. The new chief of police cracked down on the drug dealers that sold drugs in the area. Most of the hustlers that used to occupy the block either went to jail or relocated because the block was too hot to hustle on.

"This nigga needs to hurry up so I can spill his guts," E-Moe said wiping his Rambo knife down with his shirt.

"We first got to find out what Stylez told that nigga Stone."

"Yeah, then after that he's going face down in the dirt." Velli knew by that statement that E-Moe was going to give Stylez the same fate he gave Bugga. "Here he comes right now," E-Moe said holding the door open for Stylez.

Stylez damn near jumped out of his skin at the way E-Moe hopped out the car and seeing the way his pupils were dilated was an indication that E-Moe was high off PCP and that was when he was at his worst.

"Damn," Stylez whispered to himself.

Stylez got in the car and buckled his seat belt. E-Moe got in the car and sat behind Stylez. Velli pulled away from the curb. After driving a few blocks away, the silence was killing Stylez and for some reason he felt that E-Moe sitting behind him with a gun pointed at the back of his head.

"Slim I know you both fucked up at me about how I froze up at the McDonald's," Stylez stumbled over his words. Velli and E-Moe remained silent. "Man, I couldn't even help you I left my gun in the car, so I ran. I thought them dreads was there to kill all of us."

"So why you stay gone for so long?" Velli broke the silence as he started driving thought the 9th Street tunnel heading towards southside.

"Man, I don't know. I was scared as shit Velli," Stylez pleaded.

"But you didn't even check up on your so-called men to see if we were a'ight."

Stylez knew that he didn't have an answer for that letting out a deep breath.

"Velli, listen. I don't know why I didn't check up on you and E-Moe."

Velli sped the car up going through a tunnel. E-Moe was too quiet for Stylez's liking.

"Aye Moe," Stylez turned around to address his man. "I know you believe me," his words were cut short seeing the big chrome .45 Smith and Wesson laying across E-Moe's lap.

Stylez knew E-Moe didn't have a gun out unless he was going to use it. Stylez knew that he just walked into a death trap. This was his last ride. He had to do something, or he was definitely going to die today. Seeing the oncoming traffic on the other side of the tunnel Stylez decided to make his move. He grabbed the steering wheel pushing hard to the left and sending the car into oncoming traffic in the other lane.

"What the fuc," was all that Velli got out of his mouth before the dead on hit with a gray Yukon.

Stylez's equilibrium was shot. He tried frantically to get the seat belt off of him. He wiped glass from his face from the shattered passenger's window. Reaching for the door handle, Stylez found that the door was jammed shut. Still fighting to focus he tried to pull himself through the shattered window.

"AGGGHHHHH!" he yelled out in pain from his right shoulder.

Looking over at Velli as he laid behind the steering wheel unconscious with a gash in his head, Stylez knew he must fight through his pain and get the hell out of there. His life was still in danger. Hearing E-Moe in the back seat calling Velli's name he knew he had to get moving. He pushed his legs and used his good arm to manage to get himself halfway out the window of the passenger side of the car. Just as Stylez was almost about to clear the window a hand grabbed one of his legs.

"Come here you bitch ass nigga!" E-Moe yelled from the back seat.

Fear jump started Stylez's body. He kicked at E-Moe's hand with his free leg. E-Moe didn't have a good grip on Style's body. He kicked at E-Moe's hand with his free leg. E-Moe didn't have a good grip on Stylez's leg. Stylez fell to the warm asphalt of the 9th Street tunnel. Rolling over on his knees and pushing himself up to his feet he started running through the tunnel heading to the southeast side of the city.

E-Moe felt pain in his hip, but he could still move. Opening the back door E-Moe stumbled out of the car and made his way around to the driver's side. People started pulling over to see if they could help. E-Moe knew he had to move fast opening the door where Velli still laid unconscious.

"Velli!" E-Moe called his comrade's name.

Seeing the blood running from Velli's head he knew that Velli was in trouble. He could see Velli was still breathing as his chest rose up and down in a labored rhythm. E-Moe searched Velli's body but was unable to find the gun on him. He started looking around on the floor of the car. Under the seat he could see the handle of Velli's gun. He grabbed the gun and put it in his pocket.

"Baby do you need some help?" and elderly lady asked as she walked up behind E-Moe.

"Naw but help my friend," E-Moe said as he took off limping through the tunnel.

Chapter 27

"OMG Malaya! They got my baby!" Anya cried out.

Malaya rocked her beloved sister back and forth as she held her tight.

"I know. We going to get him back."

Anya received a text saying, *"We have Tiriq. If you call the police we will kill him. We will be in touch."* Anya didn't call the police. She couldn't afford to lose another child. Losing her daughter three years ago damn near killed her and losing another would surely put the nails in her coffin. When Anya got the text she thought it was some type of prank someone was playing on her but then she went through the office building looking for Tiriq and couldn't find him anywhere. Then she found the back door open. She knew then that the prank she thought was being played on her was a reality. She pulled away from Malaya and started pacing the office floor. Malaya sat down in Anya's chair and placed her ace in the palms of her hands. She couldn't hold back the tears any longer. She loved Tiriq and she couldn't figure out why that was happening to them.

"Anya!" Damu called from the bottom of the stairs as he stormed into BAM Publications' office with Biggz.

Anya raced towards her shouting husband. Seeing Damu at the bottom of the stairs she ran down and threw her arms around him.

"I want him back!" Anya broke down slipping from her husband's embrace and into an emotional heap on the floor at his feet.

Damu was so disoriented that he could not handle the fact that this was happening.

Bending down on one knee he asked, "What happened Anya? Tell me what happened. Tell me everything please Anya."

Anya ignored Damu's questions.

"Whoever took him sent this text," Malaya said handing Damu Anya's phone.

Damu read the text as he slumped down next to his wife.

"These bitch niggas want to play with my child. I need to find out who's behind this," Damu said with misty eyes. "Anya look at me," Damu said grabbing her face. Anya looked at her husband with a sadness in her eyes that wasn't known to a man but only to a mother that lost a child. "I'm going to bring our son home no matter what it takes. I promise you this Anya." Anya nodded her head up and down as the tears slid down her face. "But I need you to be strong like you was three years ago when A'idah died. I need that Anya right now. Is that Anya still inside of you? Because that is what it is going to take to bring our son home." Anya balled her fists tight, willing herself to be strong. Helping his wife off the floor, Damu placed a kiss on her forehead. "Be strong. We'll get him back. Whoever did this knows you," Damu said to Anya and Malaya. "Do you have any idea who may want to hurt you or get back at you?" Damu quizzed his wife for information.

"No Damu, I don't know who may want to hurt me by kidnapping Tiriq," Anya said wiping her tears with the sleeve of her abaya (Islamic gown).

"What about you Malaya?" Malaya took her attention away from her phone. She had been trying to get in touch with Velli ever since Tiriq went missing. "No Damu, I don't have a clue."

"What about Steve? All of this craziness didn't start until he popped the fuck up."

Malaya didn't say anything. She just looked at Anya. She knew Steve better than anyone.

"I don't know if Steve could do this. He doesn't know anything about me. He just got out. You said that it would have to be someone that knew me who did this. "Any just didn't want to put it in her mind that Steve had anything to do with this.

"He did find you once he got out of prison didn't he? And he came straight to this office building," Damu said looking into Anya's eyes for any clue that she felt like Steve may have kidnapped Tiriq.

"I don't know Damu. My thoughts are cloudy."

"Well, all we can do is wait right now and see what type of ransom they are going to be asking for, if they want a ransom. Until then we got to find out where Steve is," Damu said. "Do you have any ideas who is staying with?" he asked Anya.

"No, I don't know if he knows someone that stays in Florida other than me," Anya replied.

Malaya's phone began to ring, and the room fell silent. Malaya answered the phone.

"Hello?"

"Salaams sister. This is E-Moe."

Malaya's feet dropped.

"What's up E-Moe? Where's Velli?"

"It's all bad sister. He's been in a bad car accident."

Chapter 28

Little Tiriq laid across the dirty bed sucking his thumb with tear-stained cheeks. The small tv that displayed cartoons sat on a stand at the foot of the bed. Tiriq wasn't paying attention to what was taking place on the tv. He was terrified but his little mind didn't want to reveal that he was. His small body language told otherwise. Tiriq was never a thumb sucker but for some reason this brought comfort to him. In his mind he kept telling himself, "I'm not scared, I'm a big boy." Those were Damu's words that ran through Tiriq's head. Damu always told his son that big boys never get scared, only little boys do. Tiriq was holding on to his father's words. Hearing the door to the room unlock Tiriq closed his eyes tight and continued to suck his thumb. Two figures stood over him and watched him as he laid in the fetal position and continued to suck his thumb with his eyes closed.

"How long has he been like this?" the woman asked.

"Ever since we brought him here," the man with colorful eyes said.

Tiriq peeked up from under his eyelids like he did when Anya came to check in on him when he was supposed to be asleep. It was the same man that took him there. He'd never see the woman before but to him she was pretty like his mom.

"Did you do something to him?" the woman questioned.

"Hell no!" Colorful eyes lied. He slapped Tiriq earlier when he constantly kicked the door trying to get out of the room they locked him in.

"Tiriq," the woman called. Tiriq opened his eyes and stared into the eyes of the woman. "You want something to drink?" the woman asked. Tiriq just stared back at her without answering her questions. She reached out and touched his arm that bore a Spiderman watch that his Uncle Velli gave him. Tiriq pulled his arm away.

"Listen Steve. Don't put your hands on him and keep your emotions in check. We have a lot of work to do. I know this is difficult for you and you want to get back at Anya but by hurting Tiriq it's just going to slow things down for us to get that money."

"Bitch what the fuck you talking about," Steve got up in Keisha's face.

"You heard me," Keisha said as she walked away from Steve.

"When are you going to make the call to Anya for the money?"

"In a few hours," Keisha said as she closed the door behind her.

*****

Neva bobbed her head up and down on Mike's manhood. The slurping sounds that she made when she came up on his shaft made Mike's manhood grow stiffer. Just having Mike in the back of her throat made her kitty kat purr and rip with anticipated juices.

"Damn Neva. Put that head on me," Mike said grabbing the back of Neva's head and guiding her head up and down on his magic stick.

Neva was in heaven. She had a crush on Mike ever since she met him at her aunt's cookout a few years back. Back then he was Keisha's man but now he was all hers. She thought that she was hallucinating the day that she saw Mike. The word was that Kike died in a home invasion with his wife Kim. Well, that was what Keisha told her anyway. But now she knew that all the Keisha told her about Mike wasn't true because she had him deep in her throat right now. Feeling himself getting ready to cum he grabbed Neva's head with both hands and pumped himself to an orgasm.

"Here it comes baby," Mike said pumping faster into Neva's mouth.

Not letting a drop escape her mouth Neva lapped up all of Mike's love juices. Neva stood to her feet. Mike joined her and pulled up his pants that were gathered around his ankles. He relit his half smoked blunt and laid back down on the couch.

"I'm so glad that we bumped into each other," Neva said reapplying her Mac lip gloss.

"Yeah me-too babe. Do you think that we can really pull this shit off?"

"Of course. Don't nobody have a clue. When things are ready be looking for my call."

"Oh, I'll be ready," Mike said thinking about the punishment he was going to bring on Damu and Velli.

Chapter 29

Malaya cried as she walked into the hospital room of D.C. General Hospital Center where Velli laid with his head in bandages. The left side of his face was bruised black and purple, and his left eye was swollen shut. Velli looked horrible in Malaya's eyes. She had never seen her husband in such a state. Malaya's hands trembled as she gently touched Velli's bruised face. She could feel the heat emanating from his bruise.

"Hello Mrs. Williams," the voice said coming from behind her.

"Yes. Hello?"

"I'm Dr. Zeman. The nurse at the front desk informed me that you were here," the doctor in the white coat extended his hand to Malaya.

"Is he going to be alright?" Malaya asked drawing her hand back from Dr. Zeman and wiping her eyes.

"Well yes. He will be fine," Dr. Zeman assured her. "As you know he was involved in a bad car accident going through the 9th Street tunnel. He suffered a head injury to the left side of his head. We gave him a Cat scan and there are no signs of brain damage or swelling but the black and purple you see on the side of his face may be there for a while at least until the swelling goes down. And he may have a blood clot in his eye but that's normal in these types of cases. That just comes from busted blood vessels, but the blood clot will go away also." Malaya nodded letting Dr. Zeman know that she was listening and following everything he was saying. "Now the worst part of your husband's injuries are his broken ribs. He will need to remain in bed for about three weeks and it takes six to eight weeks to heal fully. During that time your husband will be in great pain, but rest is the key to his recovery."

"Okay," Malaya said still wiping her tears.

"Do you have any questions Mrs. Williams?"

"When can I take him home?"

"In a few days. We are going to keep him for observation and if everything checks we can discharge him. Right now, he is heavily medicated, and he'll be coming in and out of consciousness, but you are more then welcome to sit with him as long as you want."

"Okay," Malaya said feeling a little relief. "Oh, I want to have my husband moved to a private room."

"Okay, that's no problem. Just see the nurse at the nurses' station and she'll take care of that." As the doctor turned to leave the room he turned in an attempt to console Malaya and said, " I know that it may not seem like it right now, but your husband is really lucky to be alive."

*****

Stylez drank from the fifth of Remy Martin bottle while he hid out in the Lincoln Heights Projects in northeast D.C. Laying across his lap was his thirty shot Glock 40. He knew that Velli and E-Moe was out for blood. There was no way that he could get himself out of the life and danger situation unless he killed Velli and E-Moe and got back under the blanket of Mookie and his brother Stone.

"Fuck!"

Stylez let out a yell and slapped the arm of the recliner alarming Good the big-headed Pitbull that laid next to the recliner. Hearing the knock at the door made Goon stand at attention and growl. Only two people knew that Stylez was there his baby mama Missy and Mookie who he called an hour ago to come through and holla at him to help him find a solution to the problem that he was in.

Getting out the recliner he sat his gun on the arm of the chair and made his way to the door still sore from the car accident with Velli and E-Moe. Snatching the door open standing there wasn't who he expected to see. It was Nebo and Pebo, Stone's henchmen. He tried to slam the door shut but it was met by Nebo's shoulder. Stylez took off and made a run for it. Goon, Stylez's dog went into attack mode as the Nebo and Pebo approached. He was stopped dead in his tracks by Nebo's gun.

Boom!

Goon took a bullet to his head that was meant for his master. That gave Stylez enough time to escape out the bedroom window.

Jibril Williams

Chapter 30

Anya got off the phone with Malaya pleased to hear the condition of her brother-in-law Velli. She felt good knowing that he was going to be alright. It had been two days since Malaya went to D.C. to see about Velli but now that she knew that he was going to be alright she really needed the emotion support of her sister Anya. She hadn't been able to sleep since Tiriq was kidnapped right from under her nose. She was wondering how the kidnappers were able to do it. They must have grabbed Tiriq through the back door of the office building. But what she couldn't figure out was how they entered the office undetected. Anya's phone rung from the kitchen table. Her iPhone 6 indicated that the caller was unknown. Anya hit the speaker phone button.

"Hello," Anya said again. The breathing could be heard even louder. "Look you muthafucka bring my son back."

Damu heard his wife from the living room and ran to the kitchen where he found his wife standing over her phone that laid on the table. Stopping and standing by Anya's side Damu took over the situation.

"Who the fuck is this?" Damu said through clenched teeth.

"You will never have the chance to see your son alive again if you don't cough up $500,000," the female voice demanded.

"Okay you got that, that's no problem," Anya said without hesitation interrupting Damu before he could say anything.

"That was way too easy," the female voice said giggling.

"How do we know that our son is still alive?" Anya asked putting her lips close to the phone as if the caller had trouble hearing her.

"Oh, he is alive with his mute ass."

"Where do you want to make the switch for Tiriq for the money?" Damu jumped in.

"Just worry about getting the money together and I'll contract you when I'm ready to make the switch."

"Wait!" Anya yelled. "I want to know if my son is okay," she demanded.

"Okay, I'm facetiming you now."

The phone went dead and moments later Anya's phone signaled that she was receiving a facetime call. She accepted the call, and her screen came to life with the image of Tiriq laying on a bed sucking his thumb. Anya's heart hit rock bottom. She touched the screen of her phone as if she could really touch her son. A woman appeared wearing a Tampa Bay fitted cap and a red bandana around her face holing a plate of cookies. She walked over to Tiriq and handed him a cookie.

"Here Tiriq eat this." Tiriq raised off the bed grabbed the cookie from his captor's hand and placed the cookie in his mouth.

"You have three days to get that money. Remember no police," the woman said pulling out a gun and pointing it to Tiriq's small head. The screen o the iPhone went black.

Anya raced to the bedroom opened the closet, grabbed two large duffel bags, and threw them on the bed. Going over to the family portrait of her, Damu and Tiriq that hung up on the wall, Anya placed her thumb on Tiriq's right eye. Moments later you could hear a beep and air compression sounds coming from the wall. The wall that the portrait hung on pushed back and slid to the side. A small walk-in closet was revealed. The closet held a large safe and a wall full of artillery. Anya opened the safe and began dumping money into the bag.

Chapter 31

Keisha pulled the bandana from around her face and walked over to Steve to kiss him.

"Baby we are halfway there."

She stuck her tongue in his mouth and grabbed his face. Steve was unsure that this was going to work. He would have like it better if they had just set out to kill Anya and Damu.

"You really think that this is going to work huh? You really think that Anya is not going to call the Feds?"

"Trust me," Keisha said between kisses.

"Do you really think that she really got that kind of money?"

"Yeah I think that she got the $500,000 and then some. She is going to bring that bread straight to us with no problem. Anya lost one child and she'll do anything by any means to keep this one alive even if it means sacrificing her own life."

It made sense to Steve, but he was from the old school and if it wasn't rough it wasn't right.

"Aye bruh!" D-Money called from the living room.

"Yeah?" Steve answered as he and Keisha walked out the living room.

"What's good my nigga?" D-Money gave his brother some dap.

"Ain't shit, just hoping that this situation goes the way it is supposed to," Steve said eyeing Keisha.

"Baby girl got shit under control don't you Keisha?"

"And you know this."

Keisha put her hands on her hips and batted her long face eyelashes. Keisha was nobody's fool, and she knew that niggas don't let a bitch take the lead on a half million dollar move unless they plan to double cross her in the end.

"What's up everybody?" Neva said walking into the house feeling new as ever after coming from seeing Mike and having her pussy beat up nice and good.

"Where the fuck you been?" D-Money asked with his face all twisted.

"Minding my fucking business," Neva shot back.

D-Money put claims on Neva. He was feeling the young beauty.

Keisha just shook her head at the power of pussy. D-Money had caught feelings for Neva, and it was showing.

"Look don't start that shit. We got to get our shit together. I already made the call about the money. We are going to give them three days to get the money together then we are going to make the trade for it," Keisha instructed. "We don't need nothing clouding our thoughts."

"That's what's Gucci," D-Money said.

Steve moved his head up and down in agreement.

"Here's a list of things we need from the store," Keisha handed Neva a piece of paper. "D-Money go with her. Me and Steve got some business to handle so take your time," Keisha said licking her lips at Steve.

*****

Pulling up at the Walmart, Neva was tired of D-Money questioning her. She would have never listened to Keisha and gave him some pussy, but Keisha insisted that she did and now look at his lovesick ass. Getting out of the car Neva began to walk towards the Walmart entrance. D-Money jumped out and ran in front of her blocking her path.

"Listen lil mama. I'm sorry for pressing you but I am feeling you though. I think that we can have a life together."

"Weak ass nigga," Neva thought to herself. She knew that she had no other choice but to play her role until all of this was over. "It's okay D-Money. I just got a lot on my mind with this situation going down."

"I," D-Money was interrupted by Biggz who walked up with his baby mama Lady.

"Well, well look at my nigga here getting his mack on in the Walmart parking lot," Biggz stated.

D-Money cursed under his breath. "Shit, what it do Biggz?" D-Money gave Biggz a pound.

Lady looked at Neva and she knew that she had seen her somewhere.

"Ain't you Keisha's cousin that used to strip at Hollywood Nites with us about thirteen months ago?" Lady asked getting a better look at Neva. Neva was caught off guard. She couldn't do anything but nod her head up and down.

Chapter 32

Velli opened the one eye that he was capable of opening. He tried to sit up but the pain in his ribs forced him to lay back down and let out a sharp breath. His mind was groggy, and his eyes were slightly focusing in and out trying to take in his surroundings. Turning his head to the right he instantly came to the conclusion that he was in a hospital room. Looking to his left side of his bed he saw Malaya sleeping in the chair next to his bed.

"Malaya," he called out to her in a whisper.

Malaya heard her name being called and she opened her eyes to see Velli reaching out towards her. She jumped out her chair and rushed over to her husband.

"Oh baby," Malaya cried seeing her husband's one good eye opened. "Are you okay?"

"What happened to me?" Velli whispered barely getting the words out his mouth.

"Oh baby. You were in a real bad car accident," Malaya said rubbing the top par of his hand.

It all came back to Velli like a flash. He remembered that he and E-Moe picked up Stylez. Then Stylez grabbed the steering wheel and caused Velli to crash.

"Where is E-Moe?" Velli asked trying to sit up in his bed. The excruciating pain in his ribs caused him to lay back down.

"Baby you have to stay still. You have broken ribs and E-Moe is fine. He has been by here a few times," Malaya confirmed.

Velli laid there listening to his wife and letting the pain in his ribs subside.

"What about Stylez?"

"Baby I don't know anything about Stylez. Who is Stylez?" The medication still had an effect on Velli. He laid back, closed his eyes, and drifted off to sleep.

*****

"I want a small team of shooters out there when it's time to make the switch for Tiriq and the money," Damu said to Biggz.

"A'ight my nigga. We can make it happen," Biggz said pouring another shot of Cîroc in his glass.

"I want some niggas that are strictly about that gun play. As soon as we get Tiriq in our possession we airing they asses out," Damu's words slurred.

"I got two young guns from around Robert's Projects that's going to put the work in with us, Catfish and G-Baby," Biggz confirmed. "Just let me know where and when and we'll be there."

"Damn Biggz this is supposed to be your city and you haven't heard shit about my son being kidnapped?"

"Naw my nigga. Shit being quiet out here. I'm starting to think this is the work of someone from out of town."

"I don't think so Biggz. Whoever's behind this knows my wife and her publishing company. When the bitch facetimed us yesterday she called my son's name. She knows we got that kind of money. This can't be the work of someone that's from out of town. But whoever is behind this, I'm going to fill the cracks of Tampa city streets with their blood."

Chapter 33

Stylez circled the block of 14th and Belmont where his mother lived. He needed to get his money that was stashed at her house so he could head out of town to North Carolina to lay low from Velli and Stone. D.C. was too dangerous for him right now. Parking in front of his mother's house Stylez studied the dark street. He called his mom several times, but she didn't answer the phone. "She must be at bingo," Stylez thought when he didn't see her car parked anywhere on the street. Climbing out of his car he made his way to his mother's two-story townhouse. Stylez felt like someone was watching him, but he chalked it up as sheer paranoia. Nobody knew where his mother lived. He brought E-Moe over here last year sometime, but he left him in the car while he ran inside to give his mom some money for bingo and to stash a few dollars that he'd made earlier that day. E-Moe was high out of his mind off the PCP and half asleep that night he stopped by there. He didn't think E-Moe would have remembered where his mother stayed.

Sticking the key in the door and opening it Stylez walked inside shutting the door behind him and locking it. Going straight to his stash in his room he went to his mattress and stuck his hand inside the hole that was cut in the side of his mattress and pulled out bundle after bundle of money. Stylez placed the money on the bed and went to the closet to grab his army fatigue backpack and placed the money inside of it. He loved his mother so much that he wouldn't dare disappear without leaving her something to get by with while he was gone. Walking into her room he went over to her bed and placed the backpack on the bed. He took five stacks of money out the backpack and dropped it on her bed. In each stack there was $10,000.

"That should hold you over until I get back ma."

"Get back from where slim?" a voice said from behind Stylez.

Stylez turned around to stare down the barrel of Mario's 357 and standing behind him was E-Moe rocking that trademark wicked grin on his face when he was high off the PCP. Stylez swallowed hard.

"Man, I was going to take a road trip to see my family," Stylez said with worry in his voice.

"Oh, you going on a road trip but this is a trip your bitch ass ain't coming back from."

Boom!

Mario's gun roared flipping Stylez's body over his mother's bed.

"Damn you geekin ass nigga. You supposed to let me do it," E-Moe fussed at Mario's trigger-happy ass. "Let's get the money and bounce," E-Moe said.

He and Mario made their way out of the Belmont townhouse through the same back patio glass sliding door that they jimmied the lock to get in.

Chapter 34

Anya stood on the corner of 7th Avenue dressed in an all-black Nike sweat suit with $500,000 laying at her feet in two duffle bags. Her nerves were shot. She got a call last night telling her where to be with the money to get her son Tiriq back.

"You see anything Anya?" Damu's voice penetrated her ear through the hidden earpiece that she had stuck in her right ear.

"No, I don't see anything," Anya said wiping her sweaty hands on her sweatpants. Anya was hooked up to a five-way conference call with Damu, Biggz and two other people that were brought in to help get Tiriq back. Anya scanned 7th avenue with the people walking up and down the street not even aware that she had a half million dollars laying freely at her feet and that a kidnapping/ransom exchange was getting ready to take place.

Damu, Biggz and his two shooters had Anya boxed in. Damu stood in the doorway of a closed dry cleaners, hidden out of sight but with a full view of Anya. Biggz was sitting down in his truck about six cars down from Anya. The two other shooters were blending into the scenery. Suddenly a raggedy rust colored van pulled up in front of Anya blocking the view of Damu from seeing her.

"Biggz is that them?" Damu asked through the earpiece.

"I don't know yet Damu. Hold tight."

Biggz's young gun, Catfish, started easing his way towards Anya and the rust-colored van. Anya could see that it was two people inside the van. From the lighting in the streetlight provided and the position on the avenue in which she was standing made it difficult to determine who was driving the van, but Anya could tell that a female drove the van and the person that was in the back seat was a male. Anya's phone rang pulling the phone out of her pocket with sweaty palms she never took her eyes off the van that was just a few feet in front of her.

"Hello?" she answered in a shaky voice.

"You got the money?" a male voice came through the phone line.

Anya was confused. Every time the kidnappers called her it was always a woman that she talked to.

"Yeah I got the money. Where's my son?"

The door to the van opened and there sat a man holding Tiriq in his lap. Tiriq's pleading eyes met his mother's. Anya made and advance towards the man holding Tiriq. She had to help her baby. He looked so scared.

"Back the fuck up!" the mad said pulling out a gun and placing it to Tiriq's head.

Anya stopped dead in her tracks and complied with the man's commands and took her place back next to the money that was laying on the ground in the two small duffle bags.

"Oh my God Tiriq!" Anya cried out.

Hearing his son's name Damu pulled his gun, but he still couldn't see Anya. The van was still blocking the view of her. Catfish kept easing his way towards the van.

"Yo, Biggz what'chu see?" Damu asked.

"I still can't see shit. Whoever is in the van still hasn't gotten out yet."

"I'm coming to get the money once the money is in the van you'll get your son do you understand?" D-Money said to Anya.

Anya just nodded her head up and down. D-Money placed Tiriq in the seat next to him. Tiriq stared at his mother while he continued sucking his thumb. D-Money climbed out the van.

"What the fuck?!" Biggz yelled through the earpiece.

"What?!" Damu started making his way out the doorway of the store front.

"That's D-Money, he works for us," Biggz said.

D-Money walked up to Anya and had her bend down and open the duffle bags. Big faces stared back at him, and he just smiled. Anya recognized him from somewhere. D-Money grabbed the bags. He was caught up on all that money he had in his possession that he stopped being alert to his surroundings. If so he would have seen Catfish cutting between the cars. The bags were so heavy. He never knew that money could be so heavy but that was because Damu placed some red bricks in the bottom of the duffle bags to make them heavy so that when the kidnappers picked them up it would slow them down. D-Money struggled with the bags, and he had to sit one bad down and sling the other into the van. When he turned around to get the other bag of money it was too late.

Anya screamed out, "Noooooo!"

Catfish was right there, gun out and ready.

Boom!

Boom!

Catfish's 9mm opened up D-Money's chest. The woman that was behind the wheel of the van was so busy watching the man that stood in the doorway of the cleaners that she didn't even see the guy with the gun in his hand, but she heard his gun bark loud and clear. The van immediately went into motion whipping into traffic. The momentum of the van automatically forced the van's sliding door to close trapping Tiriq inside and leaving D-Money on 7th Avenue laying in his own blood.

Jibril Williams

Chapter 35

Velli and Malaya boarded the flight at BWI heading to Tampa, Florida. Malaya wanted to drive home but Velli refused to after he got the news about his nephew Tiriq being kidnapped, held for a ransom and how the ransom went bad. Velli's ribs hurt like hell. The pain in his ribs wasn't compared to what his heart was feeling at the moment. Malaya looked at her husband and reached out and grabbed his hand trying to give him some type of comfort.

"Baby Allah will work this out for us. We need to trust in him and start back fearing him as he needs to be feared."

Hearing the words of the Lord always seemed to ease Velli's mind and heart but the glare in Velli's eyes didn't soften, they just got harder.

*****

Neva's whole body shook. She had never been involved in anything like what she had gotten herself into last night. Seeing D-Money get shot was too much for her to handle. She sat on the couch with her legs up under her at Keisha's apartment listening to Steve go off about his brother.

"You stupid ass bitches go my fucking brother killed last night," Steve vented. "And your dumbass don't even got all the money. You left my brother dead in the streets."

"I had no fucking choice. The police were coming!" Neva cried and shouted back at Steve.

Keisha just leaned up against the wall with her arms folded across her chest like she didn't have a care in the world. The reason all this shit happened was because nobody trusted one another. Keisha didn't want D-Money and Steve to handle the ransom, afraid that once the money was exchanged that Steve and D-Money weren't coming back.

"I'm going to kill that little bastard in the back," Steve said making his way to the back room.

"No!" Keisha yelled blocking Steve's pathway. "We still can get the rest of the money just let me handle this shit. I'm sorry about your brother but that's how the game goes when you're out there in them streets. I'm a woman and I know how the game goes. Let's get the rest of this money and make Anya and Damu pay for your brother's death."

Steve knew that Keisha was telling the truth, but he hated to hear it coming from a woman especially a shady ass bitch like her. Steve hauled off and slapped Keisha.

"You better make this shit happen and it needs to happen soon." He gave Keisha a look to ensure that he wasn't playing anymore games. "And if this shit doesn't work out quick, fast and in a hurry I'm killing you and this bitch and I'm taking the money."

*****

As soon as Malaya and Velli's plane landed Velli gave his brother a call telling him that he wanted to meet with him and Biggz at his house about the current situation. Damu and Biggz agreed to be there in an hour.

Chapter 36

"Listen Mango, I'm going to handle Velli, and I assure you that the drugs he stole from me will be paid back in full with Velli's blood," Stone said to Mango through the phone that was being held to his ear by Splash.

Stone laid on his back in his brother Mookie's bed while Mookie's baby mother Splash rode him lightly while he held the conversation with his supplier.

"Amigo don't you know me good si? I want my dinero and Velli dead. Velli being alive is bad for business for the both of us."

"I understand that Mango and shit is going to get handled," Stone said as he looked up into the eyes of Splash. He understood why everyone called her Splash and why his little brother was so in love with this woman. Splash had the wettest pussy that he had ever stroked.

"Stone!" Mango yelled through the phone.

"Yeah I'm here Mango." Stone opened his eyes to see Splash looking at him with a smirk on her face. She knew her cookies were the bomb.

"Look me friend, get this shit done and get Velli dead."

"It will happen Mango." Stone disconnected the call.

"You like that baby?" Splash asked putting more motion in her hips.

"Oh yes baby."

Mango had contacted Stone a year ago giving hi the proposition to kill Velli in exchange for a lifetime deal on coke prices. Mango ensured Stone that his product was the best and that this was coming straight from Mexico. Stone could not resist the proposition. He looked at it like he was going to kill Velli anyway so why not jump on this deal?

Stone didn't really want to kill Velli, but Velli wouldn't let the past stay in the past and he was causing too much trouble and making him look bad in front of his brother and his city. So, in Stone's eyes, Velli left him no choice. Stone grabbed Splash's hips and bit down on his bottom lip.

"Mmmmmm, Stone you are filling me up," Splash moaned in pleasure.

Stone and Splash had been creeping around for the last nine months. Stone could have had any woman he desired but he kept finding himself in between the legs of his brother's baby mama. He decided that he would be taking Splash with him when he retired from the game.

*****

Mookie couldn't take it anymore as he watched his baby mama Splash ride his brother from the crack of his bedroom door. Mookie was feeling something wasn't right in the streets and decided to come home to get his bullet proof vest but instead he found Splash being fucked by his brother. Wiping tears from the back of his hand Mookie pulled his Glock from his waist. He couldn't believe that his brother would betray him in such a manner. Stone and Splash will pay heavily for their betrayal to him. Mookie eased the door open a few inches, but he couldn't go in. He couldn't kill his brother over some pussy, but he decided that he could betray his brother. He could make him feel the pain that he is feeling right now. Mookie backed away from the bedroom door and made his way out the house. As he was leaving he could hear Splash announcing her approaching orgasm. "I hope it was worth it bruh. I really hope it was worth it," Mookie said to himself as he crept back out the house.

Chapter 37

Velli, Damu and Biggz sat in the living room of Velli and Malaya's house. Anya was in a daze. She hadn't spoken since last night when she saw Tiriq in the back seat of that rusty van. She was sure that the kidnappers were going to kill her baby after one of Biggz's young soldiers killed one of the kidnappers. She wasn't supposed to bring anybody with her to the switch, but her husband wouldn't let her go alone. She just knew in a matter of days the police were going to find Tiriq somewhere in a shallow grave. But Damu thought otherwise. For some reason Damu thought the kidnappers were amateurs and that they would be calling back trying to get the rest of the money.

"So Biggz you say that the nigga D-Money worked for you?" Velli questioned.

"Yeah, that nigga came from out of town a few years ago. I met him through this broad we both used to fuck named Charity."

"So, the broad that was driving the van wasn't the same girl that you two was fucking?" Damu asked trying to put shit together.

"Naw my nigga that wasn't her, but it did look like the broad that was with D-Money the other night when I seen him and her at the Walmart. I can't remember the girl's name thought but my baby mama knows her. She used to strip at Hollywood Nites with her back in the days. Give me a minute let me go call my baby mama and find out the bitch's name," Biggz said excusing himself from Damu and Velli.

"I can't believe this shit," Velli said thinking about the situation that he and his family were in. Velli's ribs hurt, there were on fire. Malaya could see the pain in her husband's face. She got up to go and get him some pain medication that the doctor prescribed for him when he got discharged from the hospital. Looking at Anya Velli could see pure hurt and pain in his sister in law's eyes. His heart went out to her and Damu. He knew that his brother was trying to be strong, but the pain was all in his body language. "Something's got to give," Velli thought to himself.

"I got the broad's name; it's Neva and she got a cousin that still strips there. She goes by the name of Keisha. My baby mother said she used to mess with Mike."

Anya looked at Damu and Velli.

"Biggz, do this girl Neva have a gold Mohawk with gray eyes?" Anya asked with a groggy voice.

"Hell, yeah that's her. That's the girl that I seen D-Money with that night in Walmart parking lot. You know her Anya?"

"Yeah I know the bitch," Anya said jumping off the couch and grabbing her keys off the table. Malaya walked out the kitchen with a glass of water and pain meds for Velli. Sensing something was wrong she asked, "What happened?"

"We know the bitch that was in the van last night with Tiriq," Anya said with water in her eyes.

"Who was it Anya?" Malaya stopped dead in her tracks waiting on Anya to reveal the woman who drove the van with her nephew in it.

"It was Neva! The bitch that works for us! And that bitch Keisha is her damn cousin, the Keisha that used to mess with Mike."

Hearing Keisha and Mike's names made Malaya close her eyes. Hurtful memories invaded her thoughts. A'idah's beautiful face came to her so vividly as well as the gunshot wound to her small precious head. The thoughts of Keisha and Mike raping her was something that she lived with daily. Why wouldn't Keisha just stay away from her and her family? Hasn't she done enough damage already? Cutting Keisha's face and taking an eye out of her head and beating her within an inch of her life wasn't enough to keep her away. Right then and there Malaya knew that Keisha had to die and if she ever got a chance she would make sure that she killed Keisha.

"We have to find Keisha and Neva," Malaya said.

"We will find her," Damu said. "We will be watching Hollywood Nites tonight. And Biggz's baby mama will be keeping an eye out for her." Biggz nodded his head. "In the meantime, we will wait to see what comes up. I think that the kidnappers will be calling back. Now that we know that Neva is Keisha's cousin we know that birds of a feather flock together. That means that both of them bitches are greedy so somebody will be calling for more ransom money."

Anya prepared to walk out the door.

"Baby this is not a good time for you to be traveling alone," Damu was visibly concerned about his wife's safety.

"I'm not alone. Remember we were the two bitches that handled Keisha the first time. This will be the last time that that bitch has one up on me." Anya and Malaya walked out the door. There were on their own mission.

Damu watched them walk out but he couldn't help but smile.

"Now that's the Anya that I need right now!"

Chapter 38

Anya left Malaya's house with Malaya in tow headed straight towards BAM Publications. She and Malaya had to find out where Neva lived. Anya couldn't believe how things came back around to Keisha.

"Damn Neva is Keisha's cousin!" Anya said out loud.

"Yeah ain't that something," Malaya replied.

Anya was praying that Neva and Keisha being cousins was just merely coincidence and that Keisha had nothing to do with Tiriq's kidnapping. If so, Tiriq was in bad shape and so were they. She knew that Keisha would kill her son for sure just like she had her daughter, A'idah killed. Tears rolled down Anya's face as she pushed the truck through traffic. Reaching the office building of BAM Publications Anya pulled into the parking lot turned off the ignition and surveyed the office building and its surroundings. Getting out of the truck with Malaya Anya made her way to the front door of the office building. Unlocking the door, they stepped inside and disarmed the ADT security system. The two-story building had a deadly silence. Anya and Malaya hadn't opened up the place of business since Tiriq was kidnapped. Anya and Malaya ran up the stairs towards Anya's office. Anya stuck her key into the door and made her way to her large Cherrywood desk which held the Dell computer on it. She logged in on the computer entered her password and accessed BAM Publications' employee files. Malaya stood over he shoulder and watched as Anya scanned down to Neva Shamekia Timmons' name. Anya clicked on her name. The screen revealed Neva's application and her resume alone with a letter of reference from her college professor Mrs. Fatima Timmons. Malaya recognized the name.

"Hold up Anya. That name looks familiar. Isn't that Keisha's mother's name?"

Anya could not believe this. She hired a woman to work for her and she didn't really know who this woman was. Keisha's mother was a professor at Hillsborough Community College, the same college that Neva graduated from.

Writing down Neva's last current address Anya stuck the piece of paper in her pocket. She pulled the bottom drawers out on the Cherrywood desk removing a steel metal box. She unlocked the small box with a key that was on her key ring. The box revealed two chrome 380's with white pearl handles laying perfectly in the box. Anya picked up on e of the guns and retrieved one of the fully loaded clips. She placed it in the butt of the gun and cocked it. Next she placed a bullet in the chamber like her husband had showed her many times in the past. Anya gave the gun to Malaya and did the same with the other gun that was laying in the box. Anya placed the gun in her pocket turned her computer off and left her office.

"Let's go search Neva's office. We might find something in there that's useful," Anya said as she led the way.

Anya felt so stupid that she wasn't on point and let Neva slither her ass under her and allowed her to hurt her family. Walking into Neva's office they were confronted with the overwhelming remnants of Neva's perfume, Beyonce's Heat. She loved that perfume. Anya and Malaya thoroughly went through Neva's desk drawers, but they could not find anything useful that they could use to find Neva or that will lead them to Tiriq. Seeing the laptop still on they took a shot and touched the screen. The screen lit up and required a password to go any further. On a whim Anya typed in various words that Neva would have associated herself with heat, Chanel, Hollywood, Cîroc, bad bitch, but nothing worked. Anya slammed the keyboard in frustration.

"Tiriq mommy failed you! I'm so sorry!" Anya wailed in defeat.

Malaya needed to do something to console her sister.

"Why not try Tiriq as her password? I mean at this point it's worth a shot."

Anya looked at Malaya with blood shot eyes.

"Why not? A this point what else do I have to lose?"

"Look sis. We are in this together. Type in Tiriq."

Anya did as she was told and to their surprise the password was accepted, and they had full access to Neva's world. Malaya reached over Anya and opened up Neva's pictures that she had saved in her documents. The first picture was one of Neva and D-Money. Anya could not shake the feeling that she knew D-Money from somewhere. Clicking to the next photo there was a picture of Steve and D-Money standing side by side. The recognition of D-Money suddenly hit Anya. It's been over thirteen years since she last saw D-Money. He was a little boy back then and he went by the name Devon. Devon was Steve's youngest brother.

"That is Steve's baby brother Malaya."

Malaya was at a loss for words. The next picture momentarily stopped Malaya's heart. This can't be true but once a gain she checked the date and time stamp on the picture and confirmed what she refused to believe. Starting back at Malaya and Anya was picture of Mike asleep with Neva's naked body laying across his chest with a smirk on her face.

Jibril Williams

148

Chapter 39

"Michael, how's things going for you down in South Beach?" Mango said from the other end of the phone.

"All is good boss man," Mike said while putting some fire to the freshly rolled purp.

"Are you ready for the next shipment?"

"Yeah send it. The money will be there in about a day or two."

"Okay. Beautiful mi amigo! See South Beach is treating you wonderful. Much better than Tampa no?"

"Nothing is like Tampa to me. I took that city. I shed blood in them streets for Tampa. Tampa is mines," Mike said inhaling the purp.

"The streets of South Beach is yours now Mike," Mango cut off his thoughts.

"No, it's not. South Beach was given to me on a silver platter. They don't respect my gangsta here. They only respect me because of you. Tampa respects me, Mango. I want to go back to Tampa. I want to take my city back. Biggz don't deserve what I worked so hard for."

"No, you must stay in South Beach and handle things there." Mango could not let Mike find out that he was also supplying drugs to the same people that killed his wife and tried to kill him, Damu and Velli. "Listen to me Mike. I made you bigger in South Beach than you will ever be in Tampa."

"Yeah Mango you did that but it's not the same. At least let me seek justice in my wife's death."

"There's no seeking justice. Damu and Velli have left the country."

Mike knew that this fat muthafucka was lying but why? Why was he hiding the fact that Velli and Damu were still in the United States and moving throughout Tampa? Mango was up to something, but Mike just didn't know that.

"You know Mike there comes a time in every man's life where he just has to take a loss and let it be learning experience and keep moving."

"Yeah I feel you Mango, but I don't respect it coming from a man like you. You never let nothing go."

"Well maybe you haven't grown enough in this business to really understand the jewel that I'm trying to give you."

"Well maybe not, Mango."

Mango just shook his head on the other end of the phone.

"Amigo I have some things to do so let me go," Mango said disconnecting the call.

*****

Mango hung the phone up with Mike. He walked into his spacious spare bedroom at the far end of the hall at his west Texas home just outside of Dallas. The house was a country style baby mansion that sat and 13 acres of farmland. One of Mango's hobbies was to breed and raise horses. The house had nine bedrooms and six and a half bedrooms. The marble floors made it a dream house for any person and the Olympic sized pool the hot tub and the huge backyard were all a nice touch. Mango was stressed the hell out. He had been waiting on Stone to kill Velli. He could have easily hired a gun from Mexico but all the contract killers he knew also worked for the bosses back home and if they knew that he was wasting money to kill a man over a woman that wasn't his and not focusing on moving more product they would surely have him and his whole family murdered for his stupidity. But there was something about Malaya that made him want to risk his life. He didn't know if it was the fact that Malaya was the only woman that ever rejected him since he had been in his current powerful position. He thought back to the first time that he and Malaya were alone together.

"I was hoping that since you came here by yourself this time that we can get to know each other or at least make some type of agreement like me and your friend, Keisha had. She was very nice to me if you know what I mean. I was very good to her. You know what I'm saying?" Malaya kept her cool as Mango spoke.

"No thank you. I do appreciate it, but I'm not interested in making no type of agreement with you like that."

Mango closed the gap between him and Malaya and with a quickness grabbed her by the neck. Mango's small manhood grew hard as he thought about how Malaya turned him down. She was a challenge to him.

"No one turns me down. Nobody tells Mango no," he mumbled.

From that day forward he had been madly in love with Malaya. He even hired private investigators to follow and take pictures of Malaya doing everyday activities. He walked over to a mirror filled wall that had hundreds of pictures of Malaya. He had pictures of Malaya at Planet Fitness working out in stretchy tight yoga pants that showed nice camel toe. He had pictures of her swimming laps in her pool and laying out by the pool in her one-piece bathing suit. Mango even fantasized about him and Malaya getting married and living happily ever after in his west Texas home. Mango caught a glimpse of his naked body in a small portion of the mirror. He stopped and looked at himself. He touched the fatness on his stomach. Standing 5'3 and tipping the scale and 245 pounds with a receding hairline and a long ponytail he looked like a butter ball turkey. His eyes told the story of great hardship, and that hardship made his heart pure rotten. Standing in front of the picture where Malaya was laying by the pool in her bathing suit Mango looked on with a pornographic eye. He touched his small dangling penis as he closed his eyes and moaned Malaya's name.

Chapter 40

Anya called Damu from Malaya's phone. She was in such a rush to get out and find out where Neva had her son hidden that she forgot her phone on the living room table. She told Damu everything about what her and Malaya found out at the office. She emailed them the pictures off of Neva's computer that she found, even the one of Neva and Mike. Damu begged Anya and Malaya to come home but the ladies were on a mission. Parking across the street from the yellow and white house on Eagle View Drive in Brandon Anya checked the paper that she had in her pocket to make sure that she was at the correct address. Seeing that it was Anya and Malaya watched the house for a few minutes. They pulled their guns out of their pockets and checked them like Velli and Damu had taught them in the past. Putting the guns back in their back pockets they got out Anya's Range Rover and made their way to the house. Anya wondered if Tiriq was somewhere in this house. Malaya was wondering if she was going to have to use her gun tonight. Knocking on the door Anya waited with her hand gripped firmly around the pearl handle of the gun that she had in her pocket. Almost a full minute went by, and nobody came to the door. Anya put a little force behind her knocks this time. Malaya walked over to the front window and peeked inside the house. Malaya could see that the house was nicely kept.

Right when Malaya was going to see if the window was unlocked she heard a voice at the door say, "Who is it?" Anya stood still in front of the door with her hand still on the gun.

"This is Anya. Is Neva home?" Anya could hear the locks being turned on the door.

The door opened and she stood their face to face with Fatima Timmons, Keisha's mother, and Neva's aunt. Standing 5'5 and wrapped in a cream colored abaya (Islamic gown) and a black hijab (Islamic head garment) her brown eyes were strong and full of life. Her walnut complexion was flawless. Mrs. Timmons had aged well.

"As Salaamu Alaikum, Anya. What brings you to my house?" Mrs. Timmons asked standing in the doorway and staring into the eyes of Malaya and Anya.

"Mrs. Timmons may we come in?" Anya asked.

Mrs. Timmons looked a little hesitant, but she backed away from the door and allowed Anya and Malaya to enter her home.

"Seeing as though I offered you the most high greeting of As Salaamu Alaikum and you didn't return it can I assume that you are here to cut my face open like you cut my daughter's?" That question caught Malaya and Anya off guard.

"No, we didn't come to bring you no harm. We are looking for Neva and Keisha." Anya sized Mrs. Timmons up.

"How did you find out where I live and why are you looking for my daughter and niece?"

"How we found you is not important, and your daughter and Neva had kidnapped my son," Anya said with pleading eyes.

Malaya watched Mrs. Timmons' body language. She didn't believe what Anya was telling her.

"Listen Anya! My daughter is not capable of kidnapping someone's child. I know that Keisha has done some wild things in her sinful life, but kidnapping is not one of them."

"You must not really know your daughter then. She must not have told you that she had my daughter killed either then."

"No! Anya you and Malaya got your daughter killed. It was both of your actions that got your little girl killed. Selling drugs is not a way for the Muslims. Our good book speaks of that. Keisha told me everything that transpired between you two. Whatever happened we were to be a family of Muslim sisters," Fatima cried.

That statement touched Malaya, but Anya wasn't hearing none of that.

"Look, fuck what Keisha told you. I want my son back. Where is Keisha?" Anya asked pulling out her gun.

Mrs. Timmons gasped once she was confronted with Anya's gun.

"Anya what are you doing? Fear Allah. You come into my home with a gun?"

"Is my son here? Where are they keeping him?"

"There's no one in this house but me," Mrs. Timmons said looking back and forth between Anya and Malaya.

"Well, we're going to find out ain't we? Malaya watch her while I go check the house," Anya said as she ran up the stairs.

Malaya pulled her gun and demanded that Mrs. Timmons have a seat.

Chapter 41

Club Rose's on 10th and H Street was the most turned up spot in D.C. tonight. There were so many women in the club, some wearing their finest, some half naked and some completely naked. Mookie rented the club out for his brother Stone. He wanted to send him off in high fashion. The party was Stone's "retiring out the game" party. He spent many years ruling the streets of D.C. and now it was his little brother, Mookie's turn to shine and do his thing in the city where they loved his bother so much. Mookie convinced Stone that he should retire out the game earlier than what he had planned and give Mookie full control of the streets of D.C. and his Texas connect. Stone was kind of hesitant but once Mookie assured him that he had a fail proof murderous plot that would surely leave Velli dead Stone was all with that. Mookie told Stone that E-Moe was tired of working under Velli and that he was willing to play on a new team. Stone was happy to take the back seat and let Mookie handle things. Stone was leaving for Paring tomorrow and he was going to see the world, something that he always dreamed of doing.

It took everything that Mookie had in him not to kill his shady ass baby mother and his brother. Je just had to hold it together a little while longer and soon Stone would be gone. Club Rose's was also filled with some of Washington D.C.'s top hustlers and money getters. Niggas came from all four boroughs of the city. They came to send their man off in a good fashion. Mookie selected some of the most beautiful women throughout the chocolate city to host his brother's party. Stone sat in the middle of the club while the strippers grinded on his lap. Stone grabbed the stripper's ass cheeks and spread them apart giving the club a good view of the stripper's ass cheeks and spread them apart, giving the club a good view of the stripper's brown eye, not the one she winks out of but the one she farts, poots and stinks out of. The club cheered him and the stripper on. The hustlers made it rain on them by throwing nothing but hundred-dollar bills on them.

Splash stood there in the crowd with her face twisted up. "How the fuck this nigga gonna sit there and let that dirty ass bitch grind her stinky ass pussy in his face?" Splash thought to herself. Then she thought about it, she wasn't going to trip on Stone because tomorrow she would be in Paris with him and that dumb as bitch would still be here stripping in somebody's club. Besides, Splash knew that by the end of the night, stone would be sucking on her pussy. She smiled to herself as she took a sip of her drink. Mookie caught her dirty looks at his brother as the stripper made her ass cheeks clap in his brother's face.

"Bitch you don't even have a clue that I know that you and my brother are fucking," Mookie thought to himself as he watched Splash from the other side of the club.

Mookie felt as thought it was time to take control. He had an hour before he had to be out of Club Rose's so that the cleanup crew can get in there and clean up. Seeing that his brother was finished getting booty juice spread all over him by the stripper that just gave him a lap dance, Mookie walked over to his brother where he was chapping it up with some dudes from Barry Farms in southeast.

"Stone, let me holla at you," Mookie hugged his brother.

"What's up Slim? Thanks for the going away party." Stone's words slurred in Mookie's ear.

"It's time that I give you your going away present."

"Well give it to me then nigga." Stone smiled at his brother rocking back and forth on his feet.

"Naw not here. It's something personal so come on let's roll." Mookie led Stone out of the club.

Loyal to the Soil 2

Chapter 42

"What?! The nigga Mike is still alive?! Hell naw! I put a bullet in his chest and in his face," Velli said looking at the pictures that Malaya and Anya just emailed him and Damu.

"I don't know bruh. Maybe the nigga just lived or some superman shit like that, but I know one thing for sure we need to find that nigga and put an end to him the first chance we get. You," Velli stopped Damu from speaking his next words.

"Biggz, I know that Mike was your man, and I would understand if you wanted to cut ties with us being as though now you know that we are the ones that tried to kill him," Velli said eyeing Biggz while Damu eased his hand on his gun.

"I can feel what you are saying Velli, but the thing is my nigga that you don't realize that I had already pieced that together when Anya brought Damu to me with his unlimited supply of coke. The dead giveaway was that Anya was working for Mike, then Mike dies and then her husband pops up out of nowhere with all the coke. I just put two and two together." Velli just nodded his head up and down. "See Mike didn't give a fuck about anybody but himself. We just did business together and that's it. I'm on your team and by me having this information about Mike and still saving your brother's life should prove my loyalty to you and Damu."

The ringing of Anya's phone that laid on the coffee table broke their conversation up. Normally Damu didn't answer his wife's phone, but with the current situation and his son being abducted he hit the talk button on the phone.

"Hello?"

"You fuck boys ready to stop playing games and get me my money?" the female voice said through the phone. Damu knew that it had to be either Keisha or Neva.

"I'm sorry about the mix up we had the last time we tried to do this but that wasn't my call. I just want my son back," Damu pleaded.

"Well, whoever made that last call just cost you another $500,000 and where's Anya?"

Damu had to think fast.

"She is not well, that's why I'm answering her phone. There won't be any more bullshit. Please let me have my son. I'll give you the money that you are asking for."

Biggz and Velli listened as Damu tried to negotiate for his son's life.

"Get that money together and I will call you in three days."

"Hold up!" Damu yelled. "Please facetime me and let me see that my son is still alive."

There was a long silence then the female voice said, "Okay." The phone went dead and two minutes later Anya's phone indicated that a facetime call was coming through. Damu hit the talk button and the iPhone 6 displayed Tiriq laying on the same dirty mattress as before, sucking his thumb. He looked to be in bad shape. He was in shock of some kind. His clothes were dirty and soiled. The only thing that appeared to have life on his body was the spiderman watch around his wrist that Velli gave him.

The female wearing the Tampa Bay fitted cap and red bandana around her face appeared on the screen.

"In three days have the money with no bullshit or your son dies this time." The screen went blank.

Anya and Malaya came through the front door. Seeing Damu laying her phone back on the table she knew that Keisha or Neva had to have called again.

"What they say?" Anya rushed to Damu.

"They want another $500,000."

"Dam I wish I would have thought of this before. I know how to find Tiriq," Velli said. "The watch I gave him has a child locator in it. I had no idea that he was still wearing it. It has a GPS in it. All we have to do is turn on the GPS system and it will take us right to them. Get me my laptop Malaya."

Chapter 43

Malaya brought Velli's laptop. Velli opened it and went to a setting on the computer that Malaya had never seen before. Everyone huddled around the laptop and watched Velli work on the computer. Velli punched in a code to activate the GPS that was in his nephew's watch. A grid of the Tampa area showed on the screen then a grid of the Tampa streets appeared, and a red light glowed indicating the location where Tiriq was being held.

"Bingo! Got'em!" Velli called out as he watched the light on the laptop glowing.

"Aye Biggz, call Catfish and G-Baby up and tell them to get the fuck over here and bring their lighters. It's time to start a fire," Damu said. "Velli, where them hammers and vests at? I'm going to get my son and I'm going in there strapped like an   Afghan   soldier."

Velli escorted his brother and Biggz to the attic followed by Anya and Malaya. He pulled a large metal box away from the wall that was covered by a black sheet. Damu smiled when Velli popped the metal trunk and he saw the AR-15's, the Mack 11's and about twelve different handguns equipped with silencers. Velli's ribs throbbed but the pain meds Malaya gave him earlier helped.

Biggz grabbed the AR-15 and Damu grabbed the Mack 11 and a sig with the silencer to go with it. Anya grabbed the 9 mm Beretta with the silencer. Damu didn't say anything. He knew that Anya could hold her own better than some niggas in the streets plus there wasn't anything he could tell her to make her stay at home while he went to get their son back. Malaya didn't grab a gun because she already felt comfortable with the gun that she had on her waist that she had gotten from Anya at the office. Velli's phone ran on his hip. Checking the phone, he saw that it was E-Moe calling him. He knew that if E-Moe was calling it must be very important.

"E-Moe what's good slim?"

"Man, we need you back in the city ASAP!" E-Moe spoke from the other end of the phone.

"Slim, I'm jive in the middle of something. Can it wait?"

"Naw slim it can't wait. We been waiting too long for this Velli."

"What's going on?" Velli asked with great concern.

"The nigga Stone is trying to fly but we gotta clip his wings. I can't really explain right now but we need you here to put something on Stone's mental. That's they only way that it can be done, only by your hands," E-Moe said trying to say the least amount as possible on the phone.

Damu made eye contact with Velli.

"What's going on bruh?" Velli covered the phone.

"E-Moe got his hands on Stone, but nothing can be done to him unless I do it in person."

"Listen Velli, if it's like that go handle that business and we'll take care of the Keisha and Neva situation here. Let's kill two birds with one stone," Damu said looking at his bruh sincerely.

"Hell no!"

"Velli, you got busted ribs. If she goes bad you won't be that much help and plus I got Biggz, Anya and Biggz's two young goons."

Velli didn't feel comfortable leaving his family in a crisis like this, but he knew that Damu knew how important killing Stone was for him.

"Hey Mo, I'm on my way," Velli said and hung up the phone. "Malaya baby, let me talk to you real quick." Velli brought Malaya to their bedroom to talk in private. "Listen baby, as you know shit is getting ready to hit the fan. I need to go back to D.C. and take care of this situation with Stone that you have been wanting me to end. I hate that it came up this time when family needs me the most."

Malaya grabbed Velli's hand.

"Baby go handle your business and bring your ass back home in one piece so we can live our lives together as we have always dreamed of doing."

Velli loved his wife for being so strong.

"Okay baby, I will be right back as soon as I can, and this is over. I love you," Velli said looking into his wife's eyes.

"I love you too baby."

Chapter 44

Two hours later...

Velli was on the plane heading to Washington, D.C. He hoped that he was reading E-Moe right. How the hell this nigga get his hands on Stone alive? Velli's ribs hurt like hell. He needed some rest. He popped two more pain pills in his mouth and laid his head back on the plane's headrest and tried to allow the pain pills to take effect. Velli and Damu agreed that if he wasn't back in twelve hours that Damu and Biggz would make the move to get Tiriq back without Velli. E-Mo assured Velli that he would be back in Florida in a matter of a few hours of him landing in D.C.

"I got nine hours to do what I got to do and get on the next flight out of D.C.," Velli thought to himself. The flight back to D.C. was two and a half hours. He took a deep breath and closed his eyes.

*****

Damu and Biggz turned on Mulberry Drive and drove by the red brick apartment building where the GPS system on Velli's laptop indicated that Tiriq was. They cruised by the apartment and parked on the corner. The street was dark. This part of Tampa was called the Sulphur Springs area and it was known for drugs and crime. The small street was quiet. There wasn't anybody out but a mangy mutt that was running the streets.

"What do you think boss man?" Biggz asked from the passenger seat.

Damu wasn't sure what he wanted to do. He promised his bruh that he was going to wait but his nerves were on fire. He just couldn't sit still and wait while that bitch had his son in that apartment. "There's no telling what she was in there doing to him," Damu thought.

"I think that we can take them. There's nobody that's in there but Keisha, Neva and Steve."

"Well, if it's like that then let's do it my nigga. I'm rocking for you until the wheels fall off," Biggz said.

"Hold on Biggz. Let's head back to the house and grab Anya and everybody else. This needs to get done right."

*****

Velli touched down in D.C. E-Moe was there to pick him up.

"Give me the rundown," Velli said as soon as he jumped in E-Moe's Tahoe.

"Man, you ain't gonna believe this shit. I got a call from that nigga Mookie."

"What!" Velli said looking at E-Moe like he was crazy.

"Yeah the nigga Mookie, Stone's little brother. This nigga made me a deal of a lifetime. He turned his brother over to us for a piece of the city," E-Moe said running things down to Velli.

"Man get the fuck outta here! This shit must be a setup or something."

"Naw slim, this ain't a setup. I just left there, and I got the nigga Mario sittin on them niggas until we get there."

"Them niggas? What niggas?"

"Mookie and the nigga Stone."

"What! Come the fuck on E-Moe. You telling me that you have both of them niggas and you just waiting on me?"

"Naw, I just got Stone tied up and Mookie is making sure that Mario don't kill Stone until you get there, and Mario is making sure that Mookie don't get cold feet." E-Moe laughed at the situation. Velli couldn't believe his ears.

"So, no what?" Velli asked.

"Nigga you just kill Stone's ass and get back on the plane so you can handle your business down south. Mookie only wants you to kill Stone. For some reason, he thinks that's going to seal the deal that he wants to make with us. He wants to split the city in half, he keeps the southeast and southwest and we keep the northwest and the northeast."

Velli still couldn't believe what he was hearing.

"E-Moe you bring my gun?" Velli asked.

"Yeah, here," E-Moe handed Velli his 45 Ruger.

"Well let's see what this nigga Mookie is talking about."

Chapter 45

Steve paced the living room floor of Keisha's two-bedroom apartment on Mulberry Drive. He didn't understand why Keisha gave Damu another three days to get the $500,000 in ransom. "This bitch is too damn dumb to realize that Anya and Damu already had the money on hand because Damu was too quick to give up the money when she called," Steve thought to himself. Steve took another pull of his Newport and exhaled the smoke from his lungs. Then it hit him, Keisha thought she was so damn slick. She thought she had all the damn sense. She knew that D-Money was going to be buried in the next three days. He bet that Keisha scheduled for the exchange to be made in three days because she knew that he wasn't going to miss his brother's funeral for nothing in the world. Keisha was probably going to make the exchange with Damu and Anya while he was at the funeral and dip out on him leaving him broke and fucked up. Steve got mad just thinking about it. "This bitch has been playing me the whole time," Steve thought. Walking down the small apartment's hallway, Neva almost bumped into him.

"Damn Steve. Could you sit your ass down and try to relax?"

"I'll relax when we get that mute child off our hands and get that damn money in our possession," Steve said wiping his hands over his face.

"In a few days we'll have the money, and this will all be behind us," Neva said walking over to the front door.

"Where you going?" Steve asked walking over to Neva.

"I'm just going to the front porch to get me some fresh air to calm my nerves. You're not the only one that's on pins and needles," Neva said walking out the front door onto the porch and closing the door behind her. Steve watched the door close behind Neva. He made up his mind that he was going to kill Neva, Keisha and Tiriq as soon as Neva brought her ass back into the apartment.

*****

E-Moe pulled his Tahoe under the bridge on Benning Road where the bridge connected to Minnesota Avenue. The raindrops started hitting the truck's windshield. Velli checked the clip on his gin and made sure he had one in the chamber.

"What the fuck is this E-Moe? You sure know how to pick a place to murk a nigga."

"Naw slim, this ain't my spot of picking. You know I drop them where I find them. But this is your man Mario's spot," E-Moe said with his infamous wicked smile.

Velli pulled his Nationals hat low over his eyes and got out the truck. With his gun in hand, he followed E-Moe to a utility door that was under the bridge. Walking inside that place they were overwhelmed with the smell of piss and shit. The floor was littered with beer and wine bottles, syringes, crack pipes and empty dope and crack bags.

"How in the hell did Mario find this place," Velli thought to himself.

Walking further down into the utility room, Velli could see all types of meters on the walls. The hall was tight and narrow. Coming to the end of the hall, they made a right and stopped at the back door. E-Moe banged on the door and a moment later Mookie opened the door. E-Moe brushed past Mookie.

"Where's Mario?" E-Moe questioned.

"I'm right here Moe!"

Velli heard his comrade say. Velli and Mookie locked eyes. Mookie's eyes dropped down to the .45 Velli carried in his hand.

"Let's talk," Mookie said as he stepped back from the door.

Velli gripped the .45 tighter and stepped into the room. There, hanging in the middle of the room from a thick metal pipe by his wrists cuffed around the pipe was Velli's childhood friend Stone. Velli couldn't believe that it was going to finally end like this for Stone.

Stone looked at Velli with nothing but straight fear in his eyes. Velli just stared at him for a moment, then put his gin on his hip and placed his hands behind his back and walked in circles around Stone as he swung from the ceiling. E-Moe, Mookie and Stone just looked on in silence.

"Stone, Stone, Stone," Velli said as he walked around him. "It's been a long time. I see that you are hanging in there." Mario and E-Moe found Velli's little joke funny as they smiled. "Do you know that your brother Mookie wants half of the city? What do you think about that?"

Muffles came from Stone's mouth as he was unable to speak because his mouth was gagged with a dirty rag. Velli removed the rag from Stone's mouth. Stone spit debris from the rag on the floor.

"You little bitch nigga! You sold me out for this nigga?" Stone yelled from the pipe that he was hanging from. "You betrayed me! You and Splash betrayed me!" Stone went crazy hanging from the pipe. "You weak muthafucka! You sold me out for a bitch," Velli cut Stone's words off with a swift right hook to the stomach.

"Let's talk about betrayal since we're on the subject. Why did you betray me Stone? Why you call the police and give them that trip on me?" Stone knew that one day his past would catch up with him.

"Velli you caused that! We took over that city together, me, you, and Blake. We did it together, but you crowned yourself as boss and made me and Blake your workers. I was a better leader then you. I was more fit to run the city. You care too much about others Velli. You were too weak!" Stone yelled. Velli just kept listening as he walked circles around Stone.

"What about the oath we made? Huh Stone? What about if one leads the rest should follow? What about if one should hesitate, then the others shall push him? What about if one should betray then the others shall kill him?" Velli quoted the oath as if it was written on a piece of paper right in front of him.

Stone's mind flashed back to that cold winter night when he, Velli and Blake made that oath right before they emptied their guns into the four bodies that laid on the floor. Stone knew that he was going to die tonight.

"Man, fuck you! I killed Blake. I gave the police the tip on you. I had your brother's wife killed. Fuck you Velli! Do what you need to do!" Velli snatched his gun off his hop and pointed it at Stone.

"Hold up!" Mookie yelled stopping Velli. Mookie stepped forward. "I'm going to kill him," Mookie said pulling his .357. "All these years I looked up to you and you been a rat the whole fucking time? I couldn't kill you over some pussy, but I certainly can kill you over being a rat."

Boom!

Boom!

Mookie's gun blew off Stone's chin and put a hole on his neck. Before Mookie could turn around and face Velli, E-Moe and Mario sent two shots to the back of his head. Velli just nodded his head up and down at his comrade's decision. They knew if Mookie could kill his own brother there was no telling what he would do to them in the near future.

Chapter 46

Neva stepped out on the porch and the warm air hit her skin. She was ready to get this over with. She and Mike came up with a plan to rob Steve and Keisha and take Tiriq from them so they could get the ransom money from Anya and Damu. They had plans to go to South Beach and live their life together. Well, that was the impression that Mike gave Neva. She pulled out cell phone and dialed Mike's number. He picked up on the third ring.

"Yea what's up baby girl? I'm on my way."

"How far are you?"

"I'm about ten minutes away."

"I'm on the front porch waiting for you. We'll walk in together and catch them by surprise. Please hurry up Mike."

"Alright baby girl. I'm almost here."

*****

Damu, Anya and G-Baby watched Neva as she stood on the porch and talked on her phone. Damu knew that this was their way to get in the apartment without tripping Keisha and Steve off that they were outside. Damu called Biggz on the phone who was parked three cars down from him with Malaya and Catfish.

"What's up boss man?" Biggz answered the phone.

"You see the bitch Neva on the porch?"

"Yeah, I'm looking at her right now."

"Me, Anya and G-Baby are going to drive through the alley behind the apartment then we are going to creep up on her off the side of the building. Once we get her we going in to get Tiriq."

"Alright make it happen then. Hurry up before that bitch goes back inside," Biggz said watching Damu pulled away from the curb a few buildings down from where Neva was talking on the phone.

"Listen," Biggz said. "When Damu grabs Neva makes it into the apartment, you and Malaya stay in the truck and keep a look out."

"Gotcha," Catfish said.

Once Damu, Anya and G-Baby made it in the alley behind Keisha's apartment where they saw Neva on the porch they were out their truck and moving swiftly and quietly with their guns out.

*****

"Remember the first thing I want to do when we get this money is to go on a cruise," Neva said thinking about fucking Mike on somebody's boat.

"Baby fuck a cruise. We are going to see the world," Mike said laughing to himself. "Look let me get off the phone. I'm about three blocks away."

"Okay baby. I'm waiting for you. I'm standing on the porch." Neva disconnected the call. "Come on Mike. Hurry up," Neva said to herself. Just as Neva slid the phone into her pocket three figures ran from the side of the building pointing guns at her.

"Bitch who else is in the apartment?" Damu asked through clenched teeth. Seeing Anya there with a gun in her hand made Neva piss on herself.

"It's just Keisha and Steve," Neva said with piss running down her leg.

"Is Tiriq in there?" Anya asked. Neva nodded her head up and down.

"Let's go in then bitch!" Damu said pushing towards the door with Anya and G-Baby on his heels.

Walking into the apartment Steve was caught off guard at seeing Neva come through the door followed by Damu and Anya. He never had a chance to reach for his gun before Damu sent a shot from his Sig. 45 into Steve's chest knocking him to the floor. Anya popped him two more times in the face. Their silencers on their guns quelled the gun shots. Keisha walked into the living room from the kitchen and froze. Anya walked over to her and slapped her with the side of the gun. Keisha fell to the floor in pain. Anya stood over her.

"Where's my fucking son?"

"He's in the back room." Anya took off down the hall towards the bedroom. Reaching the room and opening the door she found Tiriq laying there on a bed sucking his thumb.

"Tiriq!" Anya called out to her son and rushed over to wrap her arms around him. Tiriq pulled his thumb out of his mouth and spoke his first words to his mother.

"Mommy I want to go home."

Anya picked him up and made her way to the living room.

"Mommy is going to take you home baby."

Chapter 47

Mike turned on Mulberry Drive and drove by Keisha's apartment. He saw Anya and Damu entering the apartment with Neva at gun point. Rage and hate jumped into Mike. He bucked at U-turn at the corner and came back down Mulberry Drive. Mike double parked on the other side of the street in front of Neva's apartment building. He got out his car and opened the back door of his caddie, pulled out a seventy-five round choppa and opened fire in the middle of the street. Yak-Yak-Yak-Yak-Yak-Yak-Yak-Yak-Yak-Yak-Yak-Yak. The Ak-47 jumped hard in Mike's hands knocking brick out of the apartment walls and sending hot rounds through the apartment.

*****

Coming from down the hall with Tiriq, Anya barely took two steps into the living room before a rain of bullets assaulted the apartment from outside. G-Baby caught a bullet to his back and neck. Damu made a run towards Anya and Tiriq knocking them to the floor and covering them with his body. Neva got hit in her stomach her insides opened up and painted the wall red with her blood. Keisha crawled to the back door and made her way out from the barrage of bullets.

*****

Biggz saw Mike in the middle of the street humping that chopper like he was in Vietnam.

"Malaya get out the truck!" Biggz yelled.

Malaya wasted no time jumping out of the back of the truck and onto the sidewalk. Biggz threw the truck into gear and floored it. Mike was so engrossed in sending bullets into the apartment that he didn't even notice the SUV coming his way. Pressing harder on the gas the truck accelerated to about 60 mph. The truck made contact with Mike sending him flying into the air. The AK-47 flew from his hands. Biggz stopped the truck and Catfish jumped out and put five shots in Mike's head. Malaya caught some movement from behind the apartment buildings. Keisha was running, trying to get away. Malaya took off running behind her. She was tired of all the drama Keisha brought into her life. She wasn't going to let her getaway.

"Keisha!" Malaya yelled out chasing behind her.

Keisha continued to run through the alley making it about three blocks away before she peeked over her shoulder realizing the female figure behind her was still chasing her. Keisha realized that she had her twenty-five automatic in her pocket so she stopped running.

Malaya saw that Keisha stopped running and she picked up her pace to catch up with her.

"It's over, Keisha," Malaya said walking up on Keisha and pointing her pearl handled chrome .380. "It stops here dammit!" Once Keisha realized that it was Malaya chasing her it increased her bravery.

"Bitch you chasing me with a gun?! Bitch you know you not going to use it. I'll take that gun just like I took your pussy," Keisha said stepping closer to Malaya easing her hand in her pocket.

"Keisha why? Why all the hate?" Malaya asked. Before Keisha could reply she said, "Don't worry about it. I'm making the sacrifice for my family, so you'll never hurt them again."

Keisha saw something in Malaya's eyes that told her that she was going to die that night if she didn't make a move for her gun. Keisha pulled the gun out her pocket with lightning speed and pulled the trigger. The gun didn't go off. She forgot to put one in the chamber, but Malaya didn't.

Malaya whispered, "Allahu Akbar," and pulled the trigger putting a hole in Keisha's head. She immediately heard scores of feet striking the pavement.

"Freeze! Drop the gun! Lay down on the ground!"

Jibril Williams

Chapter 48

"This is Angelia McClanahan with Channel 8 News coming to deliver you this breaking story. We standing in front of the Hillsborough County Jail where a Muslim woman is being held after she viciously shot another woman by the name of Keisha Leanna Timmons. Detectives on the scene reported that Timmons was shot at point blank range in the face in front of a Hillsborough County police officer, Bernard Grant. Now this Muslim woman is set to make her first court appearance this morning. We have Officer Grant here who was the only eyewitness to Mrs. Timmons' murder. Mr. Grant could you please tell us what you witnessed when Mrs. Timmons was shot?" McClanahan asked leaning her Channel 8 microphone closer to Officer Grant.

"Well, I cannot answer that at this time. There's still is an ongoing investigation."

"Is it true that Keisha was shot two to three streets over from where she lives?"

"Yes Ms. McClanahan. That is true."

"My sources tell me that there was a triple homicide committed at the victim's apartment and that the suspect may have committed those murders also?" Mr. Grant fidgeted in front of the camera.

"At this time, I can't confirm that the woman that's being held at the local jail had anything to do with the triple homicide that took place on Mulberry Drive."

"Could you please tell us the identity of the woman who you saw shoot Mrs. Timmons?"

"Yes her name is Malaya Williams. She is a resident of Wesley Chapel, Florida and she is married."

"Do you think that this was on ISIS attack that was acted out by Malaya Williams?"

"At this point no. We don't think it was an ISIS attack, but the investigation is ongoing. Mrs. Williams is due in court at 9:30 am this morning."

"Okay, there you have it. Coming live from Channel 8 News with Angelia McClanahan."

*****

Velli watched the morning news with tears threatening to fall from his eyes and venom in his heart. Malaya, his wife, was in jail facing murder charges. Velli felt like the biggest loser ever. Once again he failed to protect his wife and keep her out of harm's way. He should have never taken that last minute trip back to D.C. to handle that situation with Stone. Velli placed his head in the palms of his hands and let out a deep sigh.

Damu could feel the tension in the room and if he and Velli didn't have the same blood flowing through their veins, surely he would be dead. "Aye bruh. My nigga, I'm sorry," Damu said from his leather sofa from across the living room.

"Sorry don't get my wife out of jail. Sorry doesn't stop my wife from spending the rest of her life in a jail cell." Damu couldn't say anything. He put his head down and focused on a piece of lint that was on his plush black carpet. "Why would you take my wife on a ransom exchange with you?" Velli asked still holding his head in his hands.

"Bruh I told you before she wouldn't let us leave without her. She went crazy when I told her no. I was only thinking about getting my son out of the bands of that bitch Keisha and her sidekick, Steve. I didn't think shit was going to go down the way that it did. I didn't even know that Malaya was strapped. She was supposed to stay in the truck bruh, but I guess when Mike came from out of nowhere spitting that choppa Biggz made her get out the truck so he could run

Mike's ass over with the truck. In the process, I guess Malaya saw Keisha trying to get away and chased after her."

"Look Damu, fuck all the details. We got to find a way to get my wife out that jail. I could care less what happened two nights ago. We got to find a way to get Malaya out of jail. Even if it means killing her only witness, Bernard Grant. But right now, we got to get to the courthouse and see what that judge is talking about," Velli said shaking his head.

"Alright bruh I'm rolling with you to court," Damu said heading upstairs to take a shower and get ready for his sister in law's first court appearance. "Is the lawyer going to be there?" Damu asked.

"Yeah, I had Anya wire Mr. McCullough $50,000 out of BAM Publications account for a retainer fee."

Damu stopped on the steps.

"Aye bruh I'm down to handle this shit anyway you see fit even if we have to go up in that jail and get Malaya ourselves."

Velli just nodded his head up and down as he whispered to himself, "That may be the risk we have to take."

To be continued...
Loyal to the Soil 3
Coming Soon

Lock Down Publications and Ca$h Presents assisted publishing packages.

BASIC PACKAGE $499
Editing
Cover Design
Formatting

UPGRADED PACKAGE $800
Typing
Editing
Cover Design
Formatting

ADVANCE PACKAGE $1,200
Typing
Editing
Cover Design
Formatting
Copyright registration
Proofreading
Upload book to Amazon

LDP SUPREME PACKAGE $1,500
Typing
Editing
Cover Design
Formatting
Copyright registration
Proofreading
Set up Amazon account
Upload book to Amazon

Advertise on LDP Amazon and Facebook page

Submission Guideline

Submit the first three chapters of your completed manuscript to ldpsubmissions@gmail.com, subject line: Your book's title. The manuscript must be in a .doc file and sent as an attachment. Document should be in Times New Roman, double spaced and in size 12 font. Also, provide your synopsis and full contact information. If sending multiple submissions, they must each be in a separate email.

Have a story but no way to send it electronically? You can still submit to LDP/Ca$h Presents. Send in the first three chapters, written or typed, of your completed manuscript to:

LDP: Submissions Dept
Po Box 944
Stockbridge, Ga 30281

DO NOT send original manuscript. Must be a duplicate.

Provide your synopsis and a cover letter containing your full contact information.

Thanks for considering LDP and Ca$h Presents.

NEW RELEASES

TOE TAGZ 4 by AH'MILLION
A GANGSTA'S QUR'AN 4 by ROMELL TUKES
THE COCAINE PRINCESS 2 by KING RIO
SAVAGE STORMS 3 by MEESHA
LOYAL TO THE SOIL 3 by JIBRIL WILLIAMS

Jibril Williams

<u>Coming Soon from Lock Down Publications/Ca$h Presents</u>
BLOOD OF A BOSS **VI**
SHADOWS OF THE GAME II
TRAP BASTARD II
By **Askari**
LOYAL TO THE GAME **IV**
By **T.J. & Jelissa**
IF TRUE SAVAGE **VIII**
MIDNIGHT CARTEL IV
DOPE BOY MAGIC IV
CITY OF KINGZ III
NIGHTMARE ON SILENT AVE II
THE PLUG OF LIL MEXICO II
By **Chris Green**
BLAST FOR ME **III**
A SAVAGE DOPEBOY III
CUTTHROAT MAFIA III
DUFFLE BAG CARTEL VII
HEARTLESS GOON VI
By **Ghost**
A HUSTLER'S DECEIT III
KILL ZONE II
BAE BELONGS TO ME III
By **Aryanna**
KING OF THE TRAP III
By **T.J. Edwards**
GORILLAZ IN THE BAY V

190

3X KRAZY III

STRAIGHT BEAST MODE II

De'Kari

KINGPIN KILLAZ IV

STREET KINGS III

PAID IN BLOOD III

CARTEL KILLAZ IV

DOPE GODS III

Hood Rich

SINS OF A HUSTLA II

ASAD

RICH $AVAGE II

MONEY IN THE GRAVE II

By Martell Troublesome Bolden

YAYO V

Bred In The Game 2

S. Allen

CREAM III

By Yolanda Moore

SON OF A DOPE FIEND III

HEAVEN GOT A GHETTO II

By Renta

LOYALTY AIN'T PROMISED III

By Keith Williams

I'M NOTHING WITHOUT HIS LOVE II

SINS OF A THUG II

TO THE THUG I LOVED BEFORE II

Jibril Williams

IN A HUSTLER I TRUST II

By Monet Dragun

QUIET MONEY IV

EXTENDED CLIP III

THUG LIFE IV

By **Trai'Quan**

THE STREETS MADE ME IV

By **Larry D. Wright**

IF YOU CROSS ME ONCE II

By **Anthony Fields**

THE STREETS WILL NEVER CLOSE II

By K'ajji

HARD AND RUTHLESS III

THE BILLIONAIRE BENTLEYS III

Von Diesel

KILLA KOUNTY III

By Khufu

MONEY GAME III

By Smoove Dolla

JACK BOYS VS DOPE BOYS II

A GANGSTA'S QUR'AN V

By Romell Tukes

MURDA WAS THE CASE II

Elijah R. Freeman

THE STREETS NEVER LET GO II

By Robert Baptiste

AN UNFORESEEN LOVE III

Loyal to the Soil 2

By **Meesha**

KING OF THE TRENCHES III
by **GHOST & TRANAY ADAMS**

MONEY MAFIA II

LOYAL TO THE SOIL III

By **Jibril Williams**

QUEEN OF THE ZOO II

By **Black Migo**

THE BRICK MAN IV

THE COCAINE PRINCESS III

By King Rio

VICIOUS LOYALTY II

By Kingpen

A GANGSTA'S PAIN II

By J-Blunt

CONFESSIONS OF A JACKBOY III

By Nicholas Lock

GRIMEY WAYS II

By Ray Vinci

KING KILLA II

By Vincent "Vitto" Holloway

Jibril Williams

Available Now

RESTRAINING ORDER **I & II**

By **CA$H & Coffee**

LOVE KNOWS NO BOUNDARIES **I II & III**

By **Coffee**

RAISED AS A GOON I, II, III & IV

BRED BY THE SLUMS I, II, III

BLAST FOR ME I & II

ROTTEN TO THE CORE I II III

A BRONX TALE I, II, III

DUFFLE BAG CARTEL I II III IV V VI

HEARTLESS GOON I II III IV V

A SAVAGE DOPEBOY I II

DRUG LORDS I II III

CUTTHROAT MAFIA I II

KING OF THE TRENCHES

By **Ghost**

LAY IT DOWN **I & II**

LAST OF A DYING BREED I II

BLOOD STAINS OF A SHOTTA I & II III

By **Jamaica**

LOYAL TO THE GAME I II III

LIFE OF SIN I, II III

By **TJ & Jelissa**

BLOODY COMMAS I & II

194

SKI MASK CARTEL I II & III

KING OF NEW YORK I II,III IV V

RISE TO POWER I II III

COKE KINGS I II III IV V

BORN HEARTLESS I II III IV

KING OF THE TRAP I II

By **T.J. Edwards**

IF LOVING HIM IS WRONG…I & II

LOVE ME EVEN WHEN IT HURTS I II III

By **Jelissa**

WHEN THE STREETS CLAP BACK I & II III

THE HEART OF A SAVAGE I II III

MONEY MAFIA

LOYAL TO THE SOIL I II

By **Jibril Williams**

A DISTINGUISHED THUG STOLE MY HEART I II & III

LOVE SHOULDN'T HURT I II III IV

RENEGADE BOYS I II III IV

PAID IN KARMA I II III

SAVAGE STORMS I II III

AN UNFORESEEN LOVE I II

By **Meesha**

A GANGSTER'S CODE I &, II III

A GANGSTER'S SYN I II III

THE SAVAGE LIFE I II III

CHAINED TO THE STREETS I II III

BLOOD ON THE MONEY I II III

Jibril Williams

A GANGSTA'S PAIN

By J-Blunt

PUSH IT TO THE LIMIT

By **Bre' Hayes**

BLOOD OF A BOSS **I, II, III, IV, V**

SHADOWS OF THE GAME

TRAP BASTARD

By **Askari**

THE STREETS BLEED MURDER **I, II & III**

THE HEART OF A GANGSTA I II& III

By **Jerry Jackson**

CUM FOR ME I II III IV V VI VII VIII

An **LDP Erotica Collaboration**

BRIDE OF A HUSTLA **I II & II**

THE FETTI GIRLS **I, II& III**

CORRUPTED BY A GANGSTA I, II III, IV

BLINDED BY HIS LOVE

THE PRICE YOU PAY FOR LOVE I, II ,III

DOPE GIRL MAGIC I II III

By **Destiny Skai**

WHEN A GOOD GIRL GOES BAD

By **Adrienne**

THE COST OF LOYALTY I II III

By Kweli

A GANGSTER'S REVENGE **I II III & IV**

THE BOSS MAN'S DAUGHTERS I II III IV V

A SAVAGE LOVE **I & II**

196

BAE BELONGS TO ME I II
A HUSTLER'S DECEIT I, II, III
WHAT BAD BITCHES DO I, II, III
SOUL OF A MONSTER I II III
KILL ZONE
A DOPE BOY'S QUEEN I II III
By **Aryanna**
A KINGPIN'S AMBITON
A KINGPIN'S AMBITION **II**
I MURDER FOR THE DOUGH
By **Ambitious**
TRUE SAVAGE I II III IV V VI VII
DOPE BOY MAGIC I, II, III
MIDNIGHT CARTEL I II III
CITY OF KINGZ I II
NIGHTMARE ON SILENT AVE
THE PLUG OF LIL MEXICO II

By **Chris Green**
A DOPEBOY'S PRAYER
By **Eddie "Wolf" Lee**
THE KING CARTEL **I, II & III**
By **Frank Gresham**
THESE NIGGAS AIN'T LOYAL **I, II & III**
By **Nikki Tee**
GANGSTA SHYT **I II &III**
By **CATO**

THE ULTIMATE BETRAYAL

By **Phoenix**

BOSS'N UP **I , II & III**

By **Royal Nicole**

I LOVE YOU TO DEATH

By **Destiny J**

I RIDE FOR MY HITTA

I STILL RIDE FOR MY HITTA

By **Misty Holt**

LOVE & CHASIN' PAPER

By **Qay Crockett**

TO DIE IN VAIN

SINS OF A HUSTLA

By **ASAD**

BROOKLYN HUSTLAZ

By **Boogsy Morina**

BROOKLYN ON LOCK I & II

By **Sonovia**

GANGSTA CITY

By **Teddy Duke**

A DRUG KING AND HIS DIAMOND I & II III

A DOPEMAN'S RICHES

HER MAN, MINE'S TOO I, II

CASH MONEY HO'S

THE WIFEY I USED TO BE I II

By Nicole Goosby

TRAPHOUSE KING **I II & III**

KINGPIN KILLAZ I II III

STREET KINGS I II

PAID IN BLOOD **I II**

CARTEL KILLAZ I II III

DOPE GODS I II

By **Hood Rich**

LIPSTICK KILLAH **I, II, III**

CRIME OF PASSION I II & III

FRIEND OR FOE I II III

By **Mimi**

STEADY MOBBN' **I, II, III**

THE STREETS STAINED MY SOUL I II III

By **Marcellus Allen**

WHO SHOT YA **I, II, III**

SON OF A DOPE FIEND I II

HEAVEN GOT A GHETTO

Renta

GORILLAZ IN THE BAY **I II III IV**

TEARS OF A GANGSTA I II

3X KRAZY I II

STRAIGHT BEAST MODE

DE'KARI

TRIGGADALE I II III

MURDAROBER WAS THE CASE

Elijah R. Freeman

GOD BLESS THE TRAPPERS I, II, III

THESE SCANDALOUS STREETS I, II, III

Jibril Williams

FEAR MY GANGSTA I, II, III IV, V

THESE STREETS DON'T LOVE NOBODY I, II

BURY ME A G I, II, III, IV, V

A GANGSTA'S EMPIRE I, II, III, IV

THE DOPEMAN'S BODYGAURD I II

THE REALEST KILLAZ I II III

THE LAST OF THE OGS I II III

Tranay Adams

THE STREETS ARE CALLING

Duquie Wilson

MARRIED TO A BOSS I II III

By Destiny Skai & Chris Green

KINGZ OF THE GAME I II III IV V VI

Playa Ray

SLAUGHTER GANG I II III

RUTHLESS HEART I II III

By Willie Slaughter

FUK SHYT

By Blakk Diamond

DON'T F#CK WITH MY HEART I II

By Linnea

ADDICTED TO THE DRAMA I II III

IN THE ARM OF HIS BOSS II

By Jamila

YAYO I II III IV

A SHOOTER'S AMBITION I II

BRED IN THE GAME

Loyal to the Soil 2

By S. Allen
TRAP GOD I II III
RICH $AVAGE
MONEY IN THE GRAVE I II
By Martell Troublesome Bolden
FOREVER GANGSTA
GLOCKS ON SATIN SHEETS I II
By Adrian Dulan
TOE TAGZ I II III IV
LEVELS TO THIS SHYT I II
By Ah'Million
KINGPIN DREAMS I II III
By Paper Boi Rari
CONFESSIONS OF A GANGSTA I II III IV
CONFESSIONS OF A JACKBOY I II
By Nicholas Lock
I'M NOTHING WITHOUT HIS LOVE
SINS OF A THUG
TO THE THUG I LOVED BEFORE
A GANGSTA SAVED XMAS
IN A HUSTLER I TRUST
By Monet Dragun
CAUGHT UP IN THE LIFE I II III
THE STREETS NEVER LET GO
By Robert Baptiste
NEW TO THE GAME I II III
MONEY, MURDER & MEMORIES I II III

Jibril Williams

By **Malik D. Rice**
LIFE OF A SAVAGE I II III
A GANGSTA'S QUR'AN I II III IV
MURDA SEASON I II III
GANGLAND CARTEL I II III
CHI'RAQ GANGSTAS I II III
KILLERS ON ELM STREET I II III
JACK BOYZ N DA BRONX I II III
A DOPEBOY'S DREAM I II III
JACK BOYS VS DOPE BOYS
By **Romell Tukes**
LOYALTY AIN'T PROMISED I II
By Keith Williams
QUIET MONEY I II III
THUG LIFE I II III
EXTENDED CLIP I II
By **Trai'Quan**
THE STREETS MADE ME I II III
By **Larry D. Wright**
THE ULTIMATE SACRIFICE I, II, III, IV, V, VI
KHADIFI
IF YOU CROSS ME ONCE
ANGEL I II
IN THE BLINK OF AN EYE
By **Anthony Fields**
THE LIFE OF A HOOD STAR
By Ca$h & Rashia Wilson

THE STREETS WILL NEVER CLOSE

By K'ajji

CREAM I II

By Yolanda Moore

NIGHTMARES OF A HUSTLA I II III

By King Dream

CONCRETE KILLA I II

VICIOUS LOYALTY

By Kingpen

HARD AND RUTHLESS I II

MOB TOWN 251

THE BILLIONAIRE BENTLEYS I II

By Von Diesel

GHOST MOB

Stilloan Robinson

MOB TIES I II III IV V

By SayNoMore

BODYMORE MURDERLAND I II III

By Delmont Player

FOR THE LOVE OF A BOSS

By C. D. Blue

MOBBED UP I II III IV

THE BRICK MAN I II III

THE COCAINE PRINCESS I II

By King Rio

KILLA KOUNTY I II

By Khufu

Jibril Williams

MONEY GAME I II

By Smoove Dolla

A GANGSTA'S KARMA I II

By FLAME

KING OF THE TRENCHES I II

by **GHOST & TRANAY ADAMS**

QUEEN OF THE ZOO

By **Black Migo**

GRIMEY WAYS

By Ray Vinci

XMAS WITH AN ATL SHOOTER

By Ca$h & Destiny Skai

KING KILLA

By Vincent "Vitto" Holloway

BOOKS BY LDP'S CEO, CA$H

TRUST IN NO MAN

TRUST IN NO MAN 2

TRUST IN NO MAN 3

BONDED BY BLOOD

SHORTY GOT A THUG

THUGS CRY

THUGS CRY 2

THUGS CRY 3

TRUST NO BITCH

TRUST NO BITCH 2

TRUST NO BITCH 3

TIL MY CASKET DROPS

RESTRAINING ORDER

RESTRAINING ORDER 2

IN LOVE WITH A CONVICT

LIFE OF A HOOD STAR

XMAS WITH AN ATL SHOOTER

CPSIA information can be obtained
at www.ICGtesting.com
Printed in the USA
LVHW022231210522
719400LV00013B/768